Must Love
Christmas
Cowboys

W0114402

KENSINGTON BOOKS BY HEATHER GRAHAM

Alliance Vampires

Beneath a Blood Red Moon
When Darkness Falls
Deep Midnight
Realm of Shadows
The Awakening
Dead by Dusk

The Graham Clan Novels

Come the Morning
Conquer the Night
Seize the Dawn
Knight Triumphant
A Lion in Glory
When We Touch

The Fire Series

Princess of Fire

Anthologies

In Need of a Cowboy
Must Love Christmas Cowboys

Standalones

Tempestuous Eden
Night, Sea and Stars
Queen of Hearts
Tomorrow the Glory

Published by Kensington Publishing Corp.

Must Love
Christmas
Cowboys

DIANA
PALMER

HEATHER
GRAHAM

ZEBRA BOOKS
Kensington Publishing Corp.
kensingtonbooks.com

ZEBRA BOOKS are published by

Kensington Publishing Corp.
900 Third Avenue
New York, NY 10022

Compilation copyright © 2025 by Diana Palmer and Heather Graham
The Perfect Gift copyright © 2025 by Diana Palmer
Christmas, Crime, and a Cowboy copyright © 2025 by Heather Graham

All rights reserved. No part of this book may be reproduced in any form or by any means without the prior written consent of the Publisher, excepting brief quotes used in reviews.

Without limiting the author's and publisher's exclusive rights, any unauthorized use of this publication to train generative artificial intelligence (AI) technologies is expressly prohibited.

This book is a work of fiction. Names, characters, businesses, organizations, places, events, and incidents either are the product of the author's imagination or are used fictitiously. Any resemblance to actual persons, living or dead, events, or locales is entirely coincidental.

To the extent that the image or images on the cover of this book depict a person or persons, such person or persons are merely models and are not intended to portray any character or characters featured in the book.

If you purchased this book without a cover, you should be aware that this book is stolen property. It was reported as "unsold and destroyed" to the Publisher, and neither the Author nor the Publisher has received any payment for this "stripped book."

All Kensington titles, imprints, and distributed lines are available at special quantity discounts for bulk purchases for sales promotion, premiums, fundraising, and educational or institutional use.

Special book excerpts or customized printings can also be created to fit specific needs. For details, write or phone the office of the Kensington Sales Manager: Kensington Publishing Corp., 900 Third Avenue, New York, NY 10022. Attn. Sales Department. Phone: 1-800-221-2647.

ZEBRA BOOKS and the Zebra logo Reg. U.S. Pat. & TM Off.

First Printing: October 2025
ISBN-13: 978-1-4201-5536-5
ISBN-13: 978-1-4201-5537-2 (eBook)

10 9 8 7 6 5 4 3 2 1

Printed in the United States of America

The authorized representative in the EU for product safety and compliance
is eucomply OU, Parnu mnt 139b-14, Apt 123
Tallinn, Berlin 11317, hello@eucompliancepartner.com.

CONTENTS

THE
PERFECT
GIFT

DIANA PALMER

To the late Cissy Hartley, who founded Writerspace and enriched the lives of all the authors she pampered. You were greatly loved. You are greatly missed.

CHAPTER 1

It had been a hell of a day already. James Tiberius Blakeney, Ty for short, was tired and half-mad. Everything had gone wrong from the time his feet had hit the floor in the morning. His ex-partner had taken off in the middle of the night months ago and married a man she'd just met—an auditor who'd done the books at the bank in Raven Springs. Ty had thought she'd be with him forever. She might not love him the way he loved her, but she loved the money.

He stared out the windshield of his late-model truck, gazing toward his sprawling cabin on a dirt road in sight of a mountain range. Colorado was beautiful. He loved all of it, but cities like Denver weren't his taste. Neither were towns, even small ones. He had to go downtown into Raven Springs occasionally to do business with the bank where his checks were wired. Other than that, he kept to himself.

He lived in the country outside Raven Springs. It was a tiny little town, but it suited him, despite the memories connected with the house that he was trying to work through. He hadn't produced anything since the defection of his girlfriend. He'd gone quiet and he drank too much when he was alone. He was far and away too depressed to do anything. Luckily, there were royalties. Lots of them. More on the way, too. When he had enough, he didn't really have to work. Or so he told himself. He knew the dangers of being out of the loop too long. He'd seen it sink other professionals like himself. It was something he'd have to consider. Well, later. Much later. He was too mired in depression to produce anything saleable anyway.

Just as he was about to turn onto the dirt driveway that led to his house, he saw a beat-up old truck on the side of the road. A young woman in jeans and a T-shirt was calling a name. Loudly. He moved in behind her truck and parked his.

She turned as he got out. She wasn't tall. She came up to his shoulder. She had short, dark, wavy hair, and eyes the color of which was hidden in the shade of an autumn-colored deciduous tree. There were tears in them.

He knew her, sort of. She was Sara Whittaker. She lived a few roads past his on a ramshackle ranch. She delivered food and did odd jobs to support herself and the little brother she'd been taking care of since her mother died a few years ago and her father passed away quite recently. Her dad drank, and when he drank, he hit her with a doubled-up belt, sometimes with his fists. He'd heard about it from the sheriff, Jeff Ralston, who was a friend.

Sad story. She loved her dad but she was terrified of him, Jeff said, and he'd been sheriff for a long, long time in Benton, up the road from Raven Springs. With her dad's death, there was no money coming in except what little she could make. She wasn't trained for anything, although she did beautiful paintings when she had any extra money. They were sold to tourists who came through in the summer and stopped by the art gallery. But that was only a little money. It was no longer summer. And her house was falling down around her ears.

"What's wrong?" he asked.

She looked up at his chin with misery claiming her face. "My little brother wandered off. I just turned my back for a few seconds, while I got my cell phone out of the truck. He went after the wuppie all by himself."

Ty blinked. He hadn't started drinking today. This was too soon for this sort of wild fantasy. "What the hell is a wuppie?" he asked coldly.

"I don't know. If you find one, will you tell me? I'm all at sea." She was looking around again. "He saw it and begged me to stop. We got out together, but I forgot my cell phone in my pocketbook and went to get it. When I got back, he'd just vanished . . . Edward!" she called. "Edward Whittaker!"

"Is that his name? Ed?"

She nodded. "Yes. He'll be five, his next birthday."

He shifted his eyes. He spotted red cloth moving. "Is the boy wearing red?"

"Yes!"

He pointed.

"Good eyes. Thanks! Ed!" She started moving through the brambles. That was when he noticed that she was wearing high boots and a long, closed denim jacket that stretched to her knees.

She knew to dress for the underbrush.

"Sis! I can't find him," called the boy.

"Well, he'll come back if he's meant for you, don't you think? Now, come on. The lawyer's waiting for us."

"Don't want to go."

"Don't fuss," she said gently. "We don't have time. Come on, partner."

She picked him up, and as she approached Ty, he saw that her eyes were light, although he couldn't tell the color. It was a beautiful combination with her dark hair and pale olive complexion.

"You said he was your brother?" he asked, curious because she had dark hair and light eyes but the child was totally blond and had blue eyes.

"We have a painting on the wall of my grandfather. Ed's the image of him. You can't discount genetics," she added with a shy smile.

As she stopped and raised her eyes to his face, he saw that they were a pale, silvery blue. Odd color, with that background of dark, wavy hair. She wasn't bad looking. And where the overcoat came unbuttoned, her nice figure was visible.

Not that he noticed, of course. He was off women.

She smiled briefly. "Thanks for helping." She hesitated. "I'm sorry, but I don't know you. We don't get out much," she added.

He had to stop and think. He had two names. One was very well-known, and he didn't want to advertise it. So he gave her the less familiar one. "Ty Blakeney."

"Oh, yes, I've heard you mentioned," she said. She hesitated. "You keep to yourself. So do we. Thanks again."

She turned and headed back toward the dilapidated truck. As they moved away, he heard the child complaining.

"But what about the wuppie, sis?"

Her reply was lost in a gust of wind. He looked up. Snow clouds were forming. Winter was coming early this year. He turned back to his own truck and drove himself home.

The lawyer was standing impatiently at the door as she and Ed got out of the truck and went to let him in.

"I'm so sorry," she said, fumbling with the key. "Ed caught sight of something and insisted on seeing it closer. I had to go and get him back."

"I have a client coming in half an hour, so we must finish quickly," he said, seating himself at the kitchen table.

"I tried to come and see you, but they said you'd be busy until week after next." She paused. "I did get an appointment for then," she added.

He ignored her, opening his briefcase. "Your great-grandfather held these papers until they were needed. He insisted that was not to be in your father's lifetime." He looked up. "Sorry."

She shrugged. "He knew all about my father. He never approved of my mother marrying him."

He could see why, but he didn't elaborate. He spread

the papers on the table. "Your great-grandfather left the property to Ed, but you'll be the executor and you'll hold the property for him until he comes of age. There's a sizeable amount of money as well, to be split between the two of you."

"Money? But he hated my father . . ."

"And loved you," he said, his voice softening just momentarily. "He wasn't going to let your father get hold of a penny, but he set plans in motion for when your father was, shall we say, no longer in the picture. He never wanted you to be destitute, and it was his great wish that you continue your education so that you could have a profession."

She sighed. "I do have one; I just didn't have the money to pursue it."

"Yes," he said, looking at her over his glasses. "You have quite a talent. I've seen your canvases at the souvenir shops. You charge far too little for them."

She grimaced. "I don't know what they're worth," she confessed.

"I do. Let me put you in touch with a gallery I know. They can advise you on how to market those canvases."

Her face lit up. "Thank you."

He shrugged. "No problem. Now I need your signature on these documents." He went on to name them and explain what each meant. By the time he was through, she was almost punch-drunk. But happy. He got her bank account information and told her that her inheritance would be wired into it soon. It was a considerable amount; well, to Sara it was, anyway.

She saw him off and went back to Ed, who was

watching television on the only old black-and-white set they'd been able to afford with her father out of work half the time and refusing to let her work.

She took in a breath. "Ed, let's see what Amazon can sell us in the way of a color TV. What do you think?"

"There's no money," he said, sounding just like their late father.

She smiled. "Yes, there is. Now there is! I can pay off the credit card, which means we can use it! Come on." She sat down and hoisted him onto her lap and opened her cell phone to the Amazon app. Then they went shopping.

Her credit card was climbing into debt before they stopped. But there was now money in her savings account, and her checking account, or there would be by tomorrow. All that, besides the very large sum of money in a separate account for Ed when he was older.

It felt good to have a little cash for a change. She bought clothes for Ed and herself. Nothing expensive, but things they could really use for winter. She bought ceramic heaters for their bedrooms and slipcovers for the sofa and easy chair.

Then she stopped, because it would never do to run out of cash as soon as she'd received it. She gave a silent thanks to the dear old man who'd always been kind to his granddaughter and her children, Sara and Ed.

* * *

The first thing Sara heard the next morning was "What about the wuppie?" in a plaintive little voice.

She rolled her eyes. "Okay," she said after a minute. "We'll have breakfast. Then we'll go look for the wuppie."

"All right!"

She was certain that there was no such thing as a wuppie. But she was going to look for one, to satisfy Ed so he'd be quiet about it. She was in a rare good mood. Things were looking up.

They stopped on the side of the road again. She got out with Ed and stood listening to the birds sing while she debated where to start looking.

"There it is!" Ed exclaimed, and started down the hill.

"No! You wait for me, buster," she said, catching his hand. "There are bears and wolves and all sorts of predators. You stick with me."

"But the wuppie . . . ?" he said. "Here, Wuppie, come here!" he called. "Come on!"

There was a rustle in the grass and, suddenly, a bedraggled puppy waddled out into their sight.

"The wuppie!" Ed sang.

"Well . . . my goodness," she managed. The dog was covered with briars and brambles. It had sore places on it, as if it had been bitten by something, and it seemed full of fleas.

"We have to take care of it," Ed said, and looked belligerent.

She agreed, but she was wondering what in the world to do. She made up her mind quickly as Ed's face fell.

"First stop, the vet," she said, and thank God she now had money for bills like this one was going to be.

She'd packed an old blanket, just in case they actually found the wuppie. She tucked the poor little black-and-tan ball of fur into it and, placing it carefully in Ed's lap in the back seat, she drove them to the vet.

"Oh, my," were the first words to come out of the temporary vet's mouth as he saw the little thing.

"I said worse words," she replied in an undertone.

The vet unwrapped the puppy and put it on the examination table. He did a quick exam and smiled. "Mostly cuts and fleas and mats," he said. "He needs some patching up and then he'll just need lots of love. This breed is known for its affection and protective abilities. You'll be happy you have him one day."

"It's a him?" Ed exclaimed.

"What breed?" Sara was asking.

"He's a German shepherd," he said.

Sara looked at him doubtfully. "He'll eat a lot."

"He'll be worth every crumb," the vet assured her. "You two live alone, don't you? A little protection never hurts. Especially in these hard times."

Sara smiled at him. "You're right, of course. Ed, we'll need a name."

"Goose!" he said.

Sara gaped at him. "Excuse me?"

"Goose! It says in my book that a goose is fierce and protects people. So, Goose."

Sara laughed with the vet. "Okay," she said. "Goose it is!"

* * *

Two weeks later, she wasn't certain she was getting the same puppy back that they'd left with the vet.

Goose was gorgeous. He had fluffy tan-and-black fur, very soft, and he was already growing. He liked to run with Ed and play with the toys they bought him. His favorite was a stuffed squeaky toy that looked like a long-necked duck. He carried it everywhere and even slept with it. He slept right next to Ed's bed, too, every night. Sara loved how those protective instincts were already showing themselves.

"Why did you call Goose a wuppie?" she asked Ed one morning.

"He was just a widdle puppy," he said. "Wuppie!"

She laughed. "So he was," she agreed, and leaned down to ruffle the puppy's fur.

She'd taken two paintings to the Benton gallery that the attorney had referred her to, owned by Charles and Delia Gray, and was told that the asking price of her paintings should be in the thousands, not in single or double digits. She'd been shocked. They told her that the quality of her work was exceptional.

She'd never thought of her paintings as anything valuable, but she went to the gallery once a week and learned how to market them online. It was eye-opening. She was invited to a show in Denver, but she hesitated.

"Why not go?" the gallery owner's wife, Delia Gray, asked curiously after Sara had delivered one of her latest canvases to the small gallery. It was out of the way, but many tourists came to Raven Springs, and the gallery did a booming business in the summer and fall, before snow started falling.

"I have a four-year-old brother and nobody to keep him, and I don't own a single dress," she said quietly. "I had a dress, but I wore it out going to church, even though I only went in cold weather."

She frowned. "Why was that?"

"I only had one dress," she emphasized, seeing that the woman didn't understand. "I only went when I could wear a coat, so nobody knew I only had one dress."

The owner's wife had to hide the anguish she felt for the younger woman. "Didn't your father know?"

"He was mostly drunk," she said matter-of-factly. "I had to fight him to go to church. He didn't believe in it. After living with him, anybody would have believed in it," she added. "It was all that kept me going. Church, and little Ed." She smiled. "My baby brother was an accident, but he's my treasure. Mama almost died having him."

The girl's family tragedy made the gallery owner's wife doubly grateful for what she had. "Listen, I'll keep Ed for you."

"Mrs. Gray, my truck won't make it to Denver and I can't afford to buy a new one. Not right now, at least."

"Is that all?" she exclaimed. "Well, I'll find you a ride with an upright person," she added when Sara looked worried. "Somebody dependable, okay?"

"If you can do that, I'll go. But I still need a dress."

"Can you afford one?"

Sara smiled. "Yes. I've been saving up. And the dress shop in town is having a sale."

"Okay. Go shopping."

"I will. And thanks so much!"

"It's no problem. If you can't find something you like, I'll loan you one of my dresses. We're the same size."

"Oh, goodness, but I don't own any high heels," Sara told her miserably.

"What size shoe do you wear?"

"A seven."

Delia laughed. "So do I. No problem about that. Forget the dress shop for now. I'll deck you out, Cinderella," she teased.

Sara let out a sigh. "Mrs. Gray, that's so kind of you . . ." she replied, choked up with threatening tears. The gallery owner's wife was such a sweet person.

"It's not hard, being nice to sweet people, Sara," came the soft reply. "So stop worrying about clothes. I even have several evening bags. You can pick one out."

Sara took a breath. "You've just solved all my problems. Thank you!"

There was a lilt in the other woman's voice. "I used to be young. I think," she added on a laugh. "We'll make you the envy of all the other women present. Wait and see!"

The night of the gallery showing, Sara was decked out in a gorgeous black-and-silver dress with rhinestone inserts. It was a loaner from the gallery owner's wife, who really was just about Sara's size. And the dress was a knockout. It came up to her ears in a Victorian swath of lace that trailed down into the bodice and outlined it down to the waistline. The skirt featured more rhinestones. She had strappy black patent high heels to wear with it as part of the ensemble. Her makeup was impeccable, applied by the gallery owner's wife. She was loaned a pair of rhinestone earrings. She looked dazzling. The silver in the jewelry was almost the color of her odd eyes.

When Mrs. Gray finished, Sara looked very different from the young woman who never wore anything except blue jeans and T-shirts.

"You'll knock 'em dead," Delia pronounced.

"You look beautiful!" Ed enthused.

Sara, in front of the mirror, was dumbfounded. "Is that me?"

A door opened. "I damned well hope so," came a deep, disgruntled voice from behind, "because I'm not driving to Denver in this rig by myself!"

"It's the wuppie man," Ed gurgled.

The wuppie man glared at him as the women chuckled.

"Ed!" Sara called. "Not nice."

"What in the world is a wuppie?" Mrs. Gray asked.

"It's a 'widdle puppy,' or so Ed tells me," she replied. She looked up at Ty Blakeney, who was drop-dead gorgeous in traditional black tie.

"Did you ever find the wuppie?" he asked.

"We did! It's living with us now."

"We named him Goose!" Ed ventured.

"Goose? What breed is he?"

"He's a German shepherd," she told him. "And he's beautiful, all cleaned up and healed."

"Shepherds are good dogs. I used to have one, years ago," he added. "Well, are we ready to go? I hate these glitzy fundraisers. The sooner we go, the sooner we can come back home."

"Should I admit that I've never been to anything glitzy in my life?" Sara wondered aloud.

"Go ahead. It will make you the only sane person there," Ty grumbled. "We'll be back when you see us, Delia," he told the gallery owner's wife.

"Okay. Don't worry about Ed. I have cartoon movies," she said in a loud whisper.

"Where's the wuppie?" Ty asked.

"Oh, we left him at home," Sara said. "In the kitchen. It's got linoleum for easy cleanups."

He just looked at her.

"Did I say something wrong?" she asked.

"You should ask why people call them German shredders."

But before she could start asking questions, he opened the door and ushered her outside and into the pickup truck.

She fastened her seat belt and looked around, fascinated, after he'd climbed in and turned on the ignition.

"What?" he asked, noting her close scrutiny.

"Does it fly?" she asked. "Because with all these gadgets, it wouldn't surprise me!"

"No, it doesn't fly. Well, not unless it's on the highway," he corrected. He pulled out onto the highway and stood on the accelerator. She could have sworn that the hood of the truck raised up and leapt forward.

She held on to her seat. "Wow," she exclaimed.

He chuckled, the only time she'd heard him laugh so far. And they were off.

Sara was shocked to discover that one of her own paintings was on offer in the gallery, which was a fantasy in chrome and glass. Never having been to such an elegant place, Sara felt like the original country hick as she wandered around with a glass of champagne that she hadn't even sampled.

"Well, visions walk!" a deep voice said behind her.

She turned, almost upending her flute, and stared at a man. He was her height, redheaded and freckled, nice-looking in a way. He was wearing black tie, like her ride, but he seemed to wear it effortlessly.

"Who are you, vision of loveliness?" he cooed, smiling.

She looked around to see who he was talking to.

He thought she was being funny, so he laughed. "That's cute. Who are you?"

"I'm Sara," she said shyly.

"Danny Hartman," he said, introducing himself. "And what do you do, Sara?"

"I paint . . . a little," she said.

He just smiled, unimpressed. Lots of people painted a little.

"What do you do?" she asked.

"I work for one of the local radio stations here in Denver," he said lazily. "I have my own morning show."

"Oh."

"Oh?" He studied her like some odd species of human.

"I don't live in Denver," she explained.

"No? Why are you here?"

"I was invited," she said.

He glanced past her at a man he knew. Her companion. He'd seen Blakeney come in. They weren't friends. "Nice company you keep," he muttered.

"Oh, he isn't company," she said, wide-eyed. "I don't own a vehicle that could make it this far. I live in Raven Springs."

He blinked. "You what?"

"I live in Raven Springs. It's near Benton."

He knew where Benton was. He scowled. "Then what are you doing here?" he wanted to know.

"The gallery invited me. On account of my painting."

"Your painting." He smiled. "You said you painted a little. I remember." He looked around. "So, which is your painting?"

"That one."

He turned his head and got the shock of his life. Her painting was a landscape. A symphony of color, reminiscent of rainbows and hellfire and angelic clouds, all mixed up in a canvas that had the touch of pure genius. His lips fell apart. "That?"

She nodded. "It's not one of my best ones. But I still like it."

"But it's genius," he said under his breath. "I saw it when I came in. I was hoping to meet the artist." He turned back to her and his smile was genuine. "You have real talent."

She smiled. "Thank you."

"Who do you study under?"

She blinked. "Study?"

"Don't tell me you're beyond artistic theory?" he teased. "Do you know anatomy and the use of light and the theories of the masters?"

"I've never been to college," she said in a small voice.

"I don't believe it," he said. "Just imagine what you could do with more training! You'd be Monet in a dress!"

She was all at sea.

Ty looked around, having finally missed her while he was speaking to the gallery owner. He spotted her with the laughing hyena of the news media and his eyes narrowed.

"Oh, dear," his hostess said. "Danny Hartman strikes again." Her glower was radiating heat. "Anything in skirts . . ."

"I'll go and rescue her," Ty said.

"Oh, dear," she said again, and in a more unsettled tone. "Now, Ty, there are a lot of breakables in here . . ."

"Don't worry. I'll maneuver him back outside if anything happens, okay?"

"You'll scare her," she persisted.

"She'll recover." He kept walking.

* * *

"I know all the professors. I can get you a scholarship, with my contacts," Danny was saying, his teeth very white as he smiled. "You only need a few lessons . . ."

"She's displaying in the best gallery in Denver," Ty interrupted. "I don't think lessons are required."

Danny's smile faltered. "Blakeney, isn't it? Or aren't you Blakeney tonight? I have so much trouble keeping your names straight."

"Really?" Ty asked, and he smiled lazily. "I don't have a bit of trouble remembering yours."

"I was just telling Sara about the college courses they have available."

"I heard." He glanced at Sara. "The gallery owners would like to talk to you about some more canvases to display."

"They could have come over themselves to ask her," Hartman said curtly.

Ty looked him up and down. "Sure." He smiled again. "But they wouldn't have enjoyed it as much as I would." He caught Sara's hand in his, making her whole body unexpectedly tingle. "See you around, Harriman."

"Hartman," he gruffed.

"Oh, is that right? Sorry," Ty said. "I have so much trouble remembering names," he added in a tone that dripped sarcasm.

He tugged Sara along with him before she got in a word to Danny Hartman. "Best to stick to your own species when you're making conversation," he imparted, loudly enough for Hartman to hear him and curse under his breath.

Sara smothered a giggle and went along with him to the gallery owners.

"Who is Danny Hartman?" she asked when they were on the way back to Raven Springs.

"A species of weasel."

"No. Really."

He glanced at her. "A radio announcer with delusions of grandeur," he said. "And a good man to stay clear of. He doesn't report the news so much as he makes it up as he goes along. He doesn't have the best reputation with women as well."

"I see."

"Why was he talking to you about college courses?"

"He said I could benefit from them. As an artist. He said they taught things like the use of light, and anatomy, and how to use perspective." She grimaced. "I've never had any formal training. I just like to paint."

"The gallery owners said that you have a natural talent, and you do." He drew in a breath. "I've heard novelists say that many were ruined because they were convinced that they needed a degree in journalism or a certificate in creative writing to do what they did. Whole careers have been sacrificed on the altar of higher education."

"I don't understand."

"College professors have their own sense of how to write," he said simply. "They impart it to students.

Often, it replaces a natural talent with a carbon copy of the professor's style."

"Oh." She hesitated. "And you think that if I study art formally, I might lose my natural talent?"

"Exactly."

"I see."

"You probably won't. But think about it," he said quietly. He pulled up in front of the local gallery owners' home. "And if Danny Hartman phones you, and he might, remember that he's always got an angle. Usually, it's one that either gives him added prestige or money."

She nodded. "Okay."

He studied her in the outside lights. She wasn't really pretty, but she paid for dressing. He frowned. He didn't like the feelings he was getting. He didn't want to walk into any new relationships for the rest of his life. He'd been burned too badly.

He turned away and came around to open her door. He walked her up to the Grays' house.

"Thanks for driving me," she said. "I don't think my pickup would have made it past Benton."

"Neither do I," he said honestly.

The door opened.

"You're back!" Ed exclaimed. "Sis, we got to go home quick! It's real late and the wuppie will be crying!"

She laughed as she picked him up. "Okay, partner, just a minute while I return my borrowed finery and get back into my old duds."

"Borrowed?" Ty asked, aghast.

She grimaced. "I don't own a dress. Well, not any-more," she said with a quiet smile, completely unaffected about telling him the truth. "Thanks again for driving me." She went inside with Ed and the door closed behind them.

Ty went back to his truck in a daze. He'd never in his life come across a woman who didn't own a single dress and had to borrow things to wear to a fancy event.

The women he knew were expensive to keep, and if they needed a dress, it had to be from a high-ticket store, and he'd be expected to pay for it.

He wondered why he'd never realized that there were women like Sara Whittaker in the world. Not that he was interested in her. Never that!

CHAPTER 2

It was very late when they pulled up at the ranch house. Ed would normally have been asleep at this hour, but because of his wuppie, he was wide-awake.

"I'll bet he missed us, huh, sis?" he asked excitedly as they walked up onto the porch and heard him barking inside.

Sara laughed. "I expect so, Ed." She unlocked the door and they walked in.

Ed ran ahead of her to open the kitchen door. She turned on the lights and put up her coat and purse and Ed's toys that he'd taken with him.

Eventually, it registered that while the puppy was making excited noises, Ed was not.

She frowned and went to investigate.

Ed looked at her with dread.

"What's wrong, baby?" she asked.

He sighed and stood aside.

She looked into the kitchen and caught her breath. Part of the linoleum was torn right off the floor. A baseboard was shredded. Goose's wee-wee pads were in small pieces.

A small throw rug had been mutilated. And the corner of a kitchen cabinet looked like the victim of a buzz saw.

"He's just a baby, sis," Ed said worriedly, trying to ward off disaster. His eyes, so like their mother's, were bright with threatening tears.

Ty's words came back to her. *German shredder.*

She could have cried. But fortunately, they had enough money to repair the damage. And he was, after all, a puppy.

So she laughed.

Ed relaxed.

"Yes, he's just a baby," she agreed. "We can fix this. But we're getting him a big crate, and next time we leave the house, he's going to stay in it." She looked down at the grinning puppy with his one floppy ear down and the other standing straight up. "You bad furry child," she chided gently while the puppy looked up at her with bright, laughing eyes and his tongue hanging out while he panted. He looked the very picture of innocence.

Then she laughed and picked him up and hugged him close. "I guess we have to expect a few surprises. After all, you're not really even housebroken yet, Goose."

"And he's so sweet!" Ed said.

"Yes. And he's so sweet," she agreed, kissing the pup's head.

So they had old Mr. Loudermilk come and replace the linoleum and fix the chewed places, and they bought a crate for Goose.

"He'll grow up," Mr. Loudermilk assured them with a grin. "And he'll be a lot of protection for the two of you. The ranch is really out in the sticks." He grimaced. "Would have suggested maybe moving to town, but I know you wouldn't hear of it," he added.

"I love the ranch. It belonged to my grandfather before it passed on to Mom. I can't imagine living in a little apartment in town. Besides," she said, "Goose needs lots of room to run. And we've got it. Wonky old fences and all!"

They had fences, all right. Fences and cattle, although not a huge herd of them, and two part-time cowboys who looked after the cattle. When they had to breed them, or vet them, neighbors came to help. Sara loved the cattle business. She was a third-generation cattle-woman and couldn't imagine any other way of life.

Painting canvases, of course, helped keep things going here. But it was not a substitute for buying and selling bulls and cows.

Ed loved it, too. He'd already participated in his first rodeo, riding a pony that had been Sara's when she was his age. The pony was old, but of a good temperament, and just the right size for a little cowboy.

It surprised Sara one Saturday to find a late-model sports car coming down the driveway toward the corral.

It pulled up next to Sara's beat-up truck and the engine died.

A man got out. A familiar man.

"Well, Mr. Hartman," Sara stammered as she went to meet him, with Ed right at her heels. "What a surprise!"

He grinned from ear to ear. Like one of those funny little dolls that you knock down and it comes right back up, she was thinking. He smiled too much. But then she hardly knew him. It was unfair to judge him when she didn't really know him.

"What brings you all the way from Denver?" she added.

"This." He handed her an envelope with a flourish. "The gallery owners were going to mail it, but I had a better idea. I'd like to do a human interest piece about you for my show. Maybe for the daily newspaper as well," he added as wheels started turning in his head. "Your painting is sheer genius. And there's a lot of money in art, as you'll see when you open that envelope!"

She stared at the business envelope in her hands. It had the return address of the gallery in elegant bold script. She scowled as she opened it and took out the check. If she'd had a chair, she'd have been sitting in it, and very quickly.

"They must have made a mistake," she began, dazed.

"Not likely," he said easily. "There's big money in art, really big money, if you have the talent. And believe me, you've got it," he added.

She was still gaping at the check.

"What's it for, sis?" Ed was asking.

She drew in a breath and looked down at him. "Well, there's enough that you can go to college and we can buy a yacht and a few Rolls-Royces, and a stable of good polo ponies . . ."

Mr. Hartman was laughing. "Not that much," he chided.

"Okay, we'll leave off the stable of polo ponies," she said, and shot him an amused glance. "But it's still a lot. A lot!" she emphasized.

"Does that mean I can have a really good soccer ball to practice with?" Ed asked.

She smiled down at him and ruffled his thick hair. "You bet you can!" Up until now, they'd only been able to afford a cheap one and not regulation size for his age. He was using an adult ball, which was inadequate for him. Too heavy and really too big. He needed the smaller size. "Maybe for your birthday next month!"

"You like soccer?" Mr. Hartman asked Ed.

"I love soccer!" came the reply. "When I grow up, I'm going to play in the world championship game!"

Sara smiled indulgently. Last week, Ed had wanted a career in baseball. The week before, he wanted to be an astronaut and go to Mars.

"Not a bad idea," the man said. "Sports stars make millions!"

Sara frowned slightly. Did the man only think in terms of money?

"So, how about it?" Mr. Hartman asked. "We can do a taped interview and maybe get a few photos for the newspaper layout. You'll get a lot of publicity. It will help sales."

She grimaced. "We're very private here," she said slowly, indicating the ranch. "And there's just the two of us. Is it wise to advertise that? I mean, there are some awful people in the world these days."

"Most people are awful," he said with faint boredom. "But if you have enough money, you can bypass them." His eyes were suddenly faraway and his expression grew dark.

She wondered why he was so obsessed with money. Maybe it had something to do with why he was so negative about other people.

"Anyway, it's not something you have to worry about right now, is it? Can we go inside and talk?" he added.

"But it's so pretty outside," Ed began.

"Dust and pollen," came the terse reply. "Besides, I could use a beer."

Sara cleared her throat. "Uh, I don't drink," she said slowly. "Sorry. There's just water or ginger ale."

He looked at her incredulously. "Ginger ale?"

She nodded.

Ed looked up and nodded, too.

He sighed. "Okay. When in Rome . . ."

"This is Raven Springs," Ed said knowledgeably.

Sara laughed out loud.

Ed was staring at her. "Huh?"

"Mr. Literal," Sara teased, picking him up. "Okay,

let's go get something to drink. I think there's some leftover chocolate cake, too."

The man made a face as they walked. "I hate chocolate."

"We don't," Sara said cheerfully, ignoring his contrary look. "Ed and I love chocolate."

"Yes, we do." Ed chortled.

Mr. Hartman just shook his head.

Later, while Ed played with the wuppie, Sara and Danny sat at the kitchen table, in the midst of the destruction the wuppie had left behind. Mr. Hartman had asked her to call him by his first name.

"You need to do something about that puppy," he said, his expression distasteful as his eyes swept the damage.

"He's just a baby."

"I can't stand little things, and I loathe dogs," Danny said.

Her eyes widened. "How about cats?"

"Nasty things to have inside. Animals belong in the yard. My ex-wife was always bringing home stray animals to take care of. I wouldn't let her keep them, of course. I've never understood why people want to give human qualities to their pets. It's insane."

"Because we love them," Sara said simply, and smiled. "I've never been without a dog or a cat. My mother was partial to cats, though. I haven't spent much time with dogs, except my grandfather's working dogs."

"Working dogs?"

"He had a pair of Jack Russells," she explained as the coffee maker announced its completion with a loud beep.

He frowned. "Jack Russells? What did they do on a ranch?"

"They put up livestock for my father." He still looked puzzled. She wanted to laugh. Obviously, he knew nothing about ranching.

"When the cattle were obstinate, and didn't want to go in new pasture, Dad would turn the dogs loose. They were trained to nip at the heels of the cattle to make them move. They don't hurt the animals, they just get them going." She chuckled. "Cows and bulls can be very stubborn and, considering their size, it's a real job to make them mind. The dogs are like an extra pair of cowboys."

"Well, I never," he said after a minute. He glanced at the counter. "Coffee's ready."

She almost called him Captain Obvious. But he was a guest, and Sara minded her manners.

She got up and poured coffee into two thick white mugs. She'd already put cream and sugar on the table. She handed Danny his.

He made a face as he noted that the utensils were of different patterns. "Nothing matches," he pointed out.

"These are just cheap odds and ends," she said, her tone a little defensive. "Mama had real silverware that had been handed down in her family for two hundred years. My dad pawned them to buy alcohol."

"We never had an alcoholic in my family," he countered, sipping coffee after wiping the lip of the mug meticulously with his paper towel that served for a napkin. Sara saw that and felt uncomfortable. They didn't have much. Even coffee was barely within her budget. She had a lot of money coming, but until she put this check in the bank or the wire came through from the lawyer about the will, she and Ed were pretty much living on credit. She wished Danny hadn't made her feel like a hobo.

"Now, your friend Blakeney, there's a man who can hold his liquor. At least, most of the time," he said in a sarcastic tone.

She liked Mr. Blakeney. He'd taken her all the way to Denver and back and repeatedly refused her offer to pay for the gas. But she kept all that to herself. It was obvious that this man and Ty were adversaries. It was far and away a better idea to stay out of the line of fire, especially when she didn't know what had caused it in the first place. But Danny Hartman here was the sort of person Sara tried to avoid. Negative people just used up what energy she had and made her feel inferior. Her father had already done a good job of that. She wasn't anxious to have someone else take over for him.

She sipped the coffee. It was good and strong, just the way she liked it. She took hers black, but she noticed that Danny put four spoons of sugar and more than a dollop of cream in his own coffee. "I liked him," she said with a reminiscent smile. "He volunteered to drive me to Denver. My poor old truck wouldn't have made it to the county line!"

"I noticed. It's a piece of junk," he said bluntly.

"Well, we buy what we can afford," she muttered.

"Blakeney is a pain to deal with," he said flatly. "He

was like that long before his fiancée ran off with another man and married him."

Her heart jumped. She hadn't expected that, goodness knew why. "He was engaged?"

"They called it an engagement, but they were just shacking up."

"For a long time?"

He shrugged. "For two years. She liked to party," he recalled, smiling with the memory. "I took her dancing a time or two. Well, Blakeney would come up to Denver on business and just dump her in any hotel he was staying in. He liked room service. She liked people. He'd go to meetings and she'd call me. We'd go out on the town while he did his thing. He never even noticed where she'd gone. Hell of a way to treat a woman," he added with rancor.

"She must not have cared much about him," she ventured. She took a swallow of coffee and had to bite her tongue to keep from crying out. It was really hot.

"She said he was great in bed and he bought her lots of expensive stuff," he said sarcastically, oblivious to Sara's scarlet blush. "Hell of a reason to live with somebody, in my opinion."

"They don't sound very compatible."

"They weren't, but the last person who pointed that out to him went onto a table backward. And the table was full of food. Blakeney got barred from the restaurant," he added on a chuckle. "Talk about poetic justice . . ."

"Maybe he loved her," Sara pointed out.

"Who knows? He's the sort of man who never lets emotion get the better of him. In years past, they called him Mr. Snow." He glanced at her and laughed. "It wasn't a compliment."

Sara thought he sounded terribly lonely, but she didn't say it out loud. Mr. Blakeney had been kind to her and Ed.

"How did you meet him?" he asked suddenly.

She laughed. "Well, Ed saw a small animal on the side of the road and insisted on looking for it. We were near Mr. Blakeney's place. He saw us and came out to see what we were doing on his property."

"Yes, well, you want to be careful about that. He carries a .45 automatic and he's been known to shoot at people who come on his land without permission."

"That's pretty much how we do things out here," she reminded him.

"You can get arrested for that."

"This is rural Colorado," she said gently.

"Yes?"

She sighed. "Things are different out West in rural areas. People don't see issues the way city people do."

"Examples?"

"In the city, if someone cuts you off in traffic or calls you names, or starts insulting you, that's likely all that will happen." Her eyes were even as they met his. "Out here, you call somebody a bad name, especially a woman, somebody's going to send you to a doctor. From what I hear, it's even worse down in the South."

He just stared at her, uncomprehending.

"Example," she told him. "There was a family at a football game in Georgia. This man sitting next to a family in the stands was loud and abusive, and used every dirty word in the book. He was yelling at the players, calling them obscene names, using profanity. The father of the family asked him very politely to stop because there were women and young children present."

She took a sip of coffee. He was waiting, his eyes wide. "So," she said, "the man threw down his soft drink and started cussing the father. Who drew back a fist like a ham and knocked the man down three bleachers in the stands. When the guy got back up, with his jaw aching and his eyes as wide as saucers, he walked back up where the family was and asked the father what the heck he thought he was doing. He said he was just cussing the man. And the father told him that down South, men don't fight each other by cussing at them. 'You cuss a man here,' he said, 'and he's going to knock you on your butt!'"

He just stared at her. "You're joking!"

"I'm not," she replied with a smile. "We had a waitress at our local café who lived in Georgia. She went to college there just briefly, and it was at a school football game that she saw that go down. Long story short, the cussing man finally apologized. He and the father shook hands and sat down. The cussing man didn't cuss anymore." She laughed. "I guess maybe sometimes it's better to stay quiet and appear dumb than to open your mouth and remove all doubt."

He chuckled, the first real laugh she'd seen from him. "Well, now I've heard it all."

"I don't know Mr. Blakeney very well," she continued, "but I think he's the sort of man who would hit only if he was pushed by another man his age."

He whistled. "Boy, does he hit," he murmured. He looked up from his coffee. "He comes to Denver on business from time to time. In one restaurant he frequents, there's a waiter. The waiter is Russian. He and Blakeney are good friends now, but they weren't always. About two years ago, the Russian made a pass at Blakeney's girlfriend and told her if she ever wanted a real man, he was available. He did this right in front of Blakeney."

"What did Mr. Blakeney do?" she exclaimed.

"He folded his napkin, told his date to hurry and finish her dessert. He stood up and smiled at the waiter, who backed up a step."

"But he was smiling," she pointed out.

"Blakeney doesn't smile. Ever."

"Oh."

"He moved before the waiter even saw it coming. Stepped forward, shot his hand out, and with one quick movement, he sent the waiter flying into the table beside them. The customers were eating cheese fondue at the time and drinking red wine." He pursed his lips. "The wine was the exact shade of the waiter's blood."

"Oh, my goodness!" she exclaimed. "Did they arrest him?"

He shook his head. "The waiter refused to press charges."

"Why?"

"For one thing, Blakeney speaks Russian, which helped calm things down when the waiter realized it. Not a lot of people are fluent in it, in that area of the city. Besides that, Blakeney is filthy rich and he has some rather alarming connections. Nobody sane makes an enemy of him. He's formidable enough on his own. But his connections are pretty scary."

"Now I'm intrigued. What sort of connections?"

"He has a cousin in the Russian mafia," he replied, and finished his coffee.

She whistled. "I'd ask how . . ."

"Best not to," he interrupted. "Even his enemies don't try him. So he pretty much does what he pleases. He likes to gamble occasionally, and he loves to fight. When he's between women, he likes a willing companion. His only scruple is that he never goes near innocent women. If he has one virtue, that's it." He shook his head. "Guy's a walking conundrum. I hate his guts. But he does have one or two admirable traits."

She moved her mug around on the table. "He drinks," she said in a monotone. "I've had my fill of men who can't turn away from alcohol."

"How so?" he asked.

She just smiled.

"I see. Barely acquainted, so we only share surface secrets, I gather?"

"Give that man a prize." She chuckled.

"Okay, then." He got up. "I have to go back. I wanted to know if you'd like to go to another party, a week from Saturday." He nodded at the envelope that contained the check. "You can certainly afford a dress, so I won't take no for an answer." He smiled again.

She sighed. "I can afford a dress. But I don't have a way to get to Denver. And I can't dance."

"No problem. I'll come and get you." He leaned down, not too close. "And I'll teach you how to dance."

He was nicer than she'd thought at first. She smiled.

It changed her face, made her almost pretty. He was glad his instincts hadn't let him down. He smiled.

"Okay," she said.

"Get something pretty. Something not black," he added firmly. "It's not a funeral."

She laughed. "Everybody talks about women needing a little black dress."

"Yes. As little as possible, as in, don't buy one!"

She stood up, too. "Okay. I'll get another color."

He glanced at his watch. "Have to go. I've got an interview soon over in Benton with a former racing star who moved here. I'll see you a week from Saturday about five in the afternoon. Okay?"

She nodded. "Okay. Thanks for asking me," she added.

He shrugged. "Not a problem. See you then."

He passed Ed, who was sprawled on the area rug, without speaking to him, and went straight out the front door.

"I don't like him," Ed said softly.

She had the same sort of feeling but she didn't put it into words. She wasn't sure why she'd agreed to go out with him. She wasn't attracted to him and she didn't really like him, but he did go out of his way to bring her check up to her.

But before she could further analyze it, the wuppie ran out of the kitchen as Ed freed him, and straight for Sara.

"Ooof!" she exclaimed, laughing as he jumped up on her and almost tipped her over.

"Bad wuppie," Ed chided.

She laughed. "I can see that we're going to need some more books on how to train dogs, Ed," she told "the little boy. "And the sooner the better!"

She'd just come out of the gallery in Benton, where she'd turned in her latest canvas to the Grays, when she ran almost headlong into Ty Blakeney. The contact, so brief, was devastating to her senses. She'd never had such a reaction to a man in her life. He set all her nerve endings tingling, so that she felt sensations she hadn't experienced since her early teens.

"Whoa," he said, righting her with big, warm hands. "Where are you going in such a flaming rush?"

"Back home," she said, "before our resident shredder takes up the rest of the kitchen floor!"

"Come have coffee with me first," he replied, and his dark eyes were solemn. "I need to talk to you."

She hesitated.

"I have no nefarious purposes," he pointed out. "Just coffee. Not even an invitation to join me in a rebellion."

She laughed self-consciously. "Are you planning one?" she asked.

"Well, not this week," he replied.

"In that case, okay. But Dutch treat," she added.

"What, exactly, does that mean?" he wondered aloud.

She frowned. "I don't know. It doesn't sound particularly kind, though, does it?"

"It doesn't. So I'll buy my coffee and you can buy yours." He hesitated. "If there's only one Danish and we have to split it, we'll work out how much each of us has to pay for that and our vanilla cappuccino on our Dutch treat." He stopped and his dark eyes widened. "We started out on coffee and now we're doing a world tour."

She burst out laughing. She'd rarely ever done that. He made her feel bubbly inside. She didn't dwell on why. It was enough just to enjoy the next few minutes.

"Okay, then," she said. "The world tour it is."

He drew change out of his pocket and counted it. "I have twenty-seven cents, a button, a gym clip, and two mints."

She did the same. "Ha!" she said. "I've got seventy-five cents, four pennies, a tack, two horseshoe nails, and a washer that goes to something, but I don't know what. I win."

He dumped what he had in his hand into what she had in her hand. "Then you're buying," he said, tongue in cheek, and led the way out of the restaurant. Several people watched them go, with much curiosity.

She grimaced as they walked down the street to the new fancy coffee shop.

"What is it?" he asked. He was wearing working gear, jeans and shotgun chaps, boots and a flannel shirt, because it was nippy.

"It's a small community. We're being watched," she said.

He sighed. "Well, if they gossip about us, they'll leave other people alone."

"I guess."

He looked down at her bent head. "Don't let gossip

worry you," he said. "You already know that small towns have people who love to talk, but it's mostly kind."

She made a face. "No, it isn't."

He shrugged. "Some of it is," he corrected. "Except that I'm secretly a vampire—or maybe a secret agent working undercover—and you're running a dog rescue or you're one of the missing people who were kidnapped by aliens and the government is hiding you here until they're ready to go public."

She stopped in the middle of the sidewalk and started laughing and almost couldn't stop.

He grinned at her.

"See how gossip works?" he asked pleasantly. "At least, how it works around Benton, anyway. I understand that in Raven Springs, you're a witch and I'm really a Slavic prince whose throne was taken away by his evil sister."

"Really? Was it?" she asked, all silver-gray eyes and curiosity.

He glowered at her.

"Just checking," she replied with twinkling silver eyes. "Where are we going?"

"There."

It was the newest coffee joint in Benton. They had the best coffee, too. Not that the Gray Dove's coffee was bad. But this shop's specialty was every kind of coffee harvested, and in many different flavors and forms.

Plus, the service was efficient and friendly. And, at this hour of the day, when most people who worked inside weren't occupying stools, mostly empty.

They ordered coffee and paid for it, then found a booth against the back wall.

Ty leaned back in his seat, his dark eyes steady on her face. She felt like squirming. It was a very piercing scrutiny.

"Is there something on your mind?" she asked finally, because she felt like a bug on a pin.

He nodded.

"What?"

"Why was Danny Hartman at your ranch?" he asked bluntly.

She stared at him without speaking. Well, it was a small town, and people did gossip. But she wondered where Ty had heard about her visitor.

CHAPTER 3

Sara's purse jumped in her hands. Fortunately she got it into the booth with her before it spilled out all her cosmetics and pocket change. She fumbled it closed and put it to one side.

"Why do you want to know?" she hedged.

He had the most piercing eyes she'd ever seen. They were very dark and very intent on her flushed face.

She grimaced. She couldn't outstare him. "He wants to do a feature story about me for his radio station and the daily newspaper in the city."

While he was contemplating that, the waitress brought steaming cups of vanilla cappuccino and placed them in front of the customers with a smile.

Blakeney thanked her, and the woman, young and very pretty, grinned and started talking to him.

It was fascinating to Sara to watch him absolutely freeze out the overly friendly waitress.

He wasn't rude. He just stared at her, a piercing gaze that could have made ice out of hot water. It was the same look he'd given Sara when she didn't want to tell him about Danny Hartman's visit.

The waitress got the message very quickly, smiled, and retreated.

"Wow," Sara said under her breath, observing him openly.

Both dark eyebrows went up in a question.

"I thought I was the only person who could do that," she explained, a little hesitantly.

"Do what?"

"Freeze people," she replied. She sipped her coffee. It was delicious, but very hot. Sara put the cup back onto the saucer. She then looked up at Blakeney, who was puzzled.

"I don't like forward men," she said after a minute. She flushed. "Well, overly friendly ones, I mean. I'm sort of out of step with the modern world."

"Do you have the problem very often?" he wondered, as if in disbelief.

She glowered at him. "Any young woman with a passable figure does," she told him. "Modern city men think anything feminine can't wait to go to their apartments with them. At night, too!"

He blinked. "What does night have to do with it?"

She sighed, shaking her head. Didn't men know anything about convention? "I've been told, by a number of people, that if a woman goes alone to a man's apartment or house, at night, that she's looking for a good time. I don't do that," she added curtly. "Not ever."

He was remembering how easily his former girlfriend had done that. And not only with him. Now he was studying Sara with intense scrutiny.

"Could you stop doing that, please?" she muttered,

averting her gaze. "You make me feel like a throwback to Victorian England."

He actually chuckled before he sipped his own coffee. "Sorry. But you sound like one." He sighed. "I'll bet you even go to church."

She glared at him. "There's nothing wrong with going to church."

"To be told that everything you do is wrong," he scoffed.

She glared harder. "The point of the thing is not to do things that are wrong. Not that many people in this modern madhouse of a decade would have any idea what that is."

He put down his cup and cocked his head. In the overhead light, his dark hair had a sheen like a raven's feathers.

"I don't like being lectured," he said quietly.

She just smiled.

He wrinkled his nose. "And don't smirk at me," he said irritably.

"I wasn't smirking," she replied.

"You were," he accused.

She sighed. "Okay. I was smirking a little. Just a little. But even you would have to admit that life in the cities is way different than life in rural Colorado."

"Parts of it," he agreed. "How's the wuppie?"

She sighed. "We got the kitchen repaired," she replied.

He chuckled again. "Told you."

"He's just a baby," she replied with a smile. "We'll teach him, and he'll learn."

"Leave him alone and you won't have a kitchen next time."

She studied him curiously. "You know a lot about shepherds."

"I used to have one," he said, and his voice softened. "Had him for thirteen years." His eyes lowered to his coffee. "Still miss him."

"I'm sorry," she said. "I know what it's like to lose a pet."

"He wasn't exactly a pet. But it's comparable."

She was dying to ask what he meant, but she bit down on the question. It was obvious that he didn't want to discuss it. She sipped more cappuccino. "Mr. Hartman doesn't like dogs or cats."

"Mr. Hartman is an a . . ."

She held up a hand. "Please. There are women and children present," she said with a grin, reminiscing about the story she'd imparted to Hartman, about what happened down South to some men who cursed in front of women.

He burst out laughing. He genuinely liked her. She had a quirky personality and she was the most straightforward woman he'd ever met.

"Sorry," she said with twinkling silver eyes. "I couldn't resist it." She sipped more coffee. "You don't like Mr. Hartman," she murmured.

"If they ever make homicide legal for a day, I'll make sure I'm in Denver when it happens," he said enigmatically.

She cocked her head and studied his hardened features. Her eyes went almost involuntarily to his chiseled mouth. Her heart skipped and she looked hurriedly away.

"You want to ask why, but you won't," he said, puzzled.

She grimaced. "I don't like to pry," she said simply. "If you do that, you lose people's respect. Besides, I don't like it when people do it to me." Her own features tautened.

"People like Hartman?" he queried with a sardonic smile.

She sighed. "Well, yes. He pries." She looked up. "I guess it's because of the job he does, but it's uncomfortable. I don't like talking about my life."

He knew why. "Your father should have been handcuffed and put in jail for several years," he said curtly.

So he knew. She drew in a long breath. Probably everybody from Benton to Raven Springs knew. Her father's behavior was notorious.

"It wasn't easy living with him."

"How old are you?"

She blinked, startled. "Twenty-four," she blurted out.

"You were of age. You could have left home."

She nodded. "But Mama was always sickly and needed nursing. Then she died and there was Ed. My father couldn't manage alone, and we had no other family that could take care of him."

"You were trapped," he said quietly.

She started to protest, shrugged, and finished her coffee. "I was trapped," she agreed finally.

"And incapable of getting out, even if there hadn't been Ed."

Her heart skipped. She just stared at him.

He leaned back against the booth, watching her. "You probably don't realize it, but there's a certain posture you see in people who've been physically assaulted."

She flushed.

"It's not something you can handle on your own," he said. "But Jeff Ralston would have helped, if you'd asked him."

She let out a sigh. "How?" she said. "If Dad had been arrested, Ed would have gone into a foster home. I was flat broke. I couldn't afford a lawyer. And even if I could have, Dad said . . ." She bit down hard on that.

He nodded. "He said he'd kill you both."

"How in the world did you know that?" she asked, aghast.

He stared into the cup in his hand. "Long life experience," he said shortly. He looked up. "I'm thirty-four. I've seen the elephant."

In other words, he'd seen the world. It was an expression she knew, from a long fascination with histories of the Old West.

She smiled gently. "I've spent my life reading histories of the western states. I understood that reference," she added, wondering if he'd get what she was saying.

"Cute," he said, and chuckled. "I loved the first Avengers movie. Captain America said that when his comrades mentioned the flying monkeys in *The Wizard of Oz*."

"You're quick," she remarked.

"I've always had to be," he said enigmatically.

She was looking at his hands. They were very steady. Where the cuff of his shirt was briefly pushed back, there was a deep scar.

He glared at her. "Some people are too quick," he said, pulling the cuff back over the scar. "And no comment."

"I don't tell tales," she said softly.

He studied her. "No. I don't think you do."

"I've had enough told on me," she said simply. "Everybody knew about Dad. I got ragged in school because of the things he did."

Her dad would get drunk and start fights at the single bar in Raven Springs. Often, the sheriff or one of his deputies would intervene and take her father home to the ranch. She'd never understood their quiet care of him. He was never arrested.

"It's so odd, the way the sheriff's department was with Dad. They never arrested him when he went brawling."

He knew why. He didn't share it. She was learning too much about him already. He didn't like it. Even his girlfriend had never reached inside him the way Sara did. The other woman liked him in bed and loved his money, but there was no love in the relationship. He'd turned his back on love years ago. It had been necessary not to feel much of anything. Emotional attachments would be found out and exploited. He became immune. But his girlfriend had caught him at a time when he was reliving painful memories, when he needed someone badly. He'd thought she cared about him. He'd thought he loved her. Now, he wasn't so sure.

He looked at Sara and thought about sharing his true background with her. Then he laughed to himself. She, with her sterling morals and quiet acceptance of whatever life threw at her, with her bedrock of faith, would never understand the things he'd had to do. So it was just as well that he had no real interest in getting to know her. Of course, he was trying to save her from Hartman. But it wasn't personal, he told himself. Certainly he had no involvement with her, and planned none.

"You want to watch Hartman," he said as he finished his coffee and put the cup down.

He had beautiful hands, she thought absently. They were big and strong-looking, with pale olive skin, like his face. He was good-looking. He seemed the sort of man who would fight through impossible odds for anyone he cared about. Fascinating, how much she knew about him, how much she learned, without words.

"What are you thinking?" he wondered aloud.

"About how much . . ." She stopped abruptly and flushed. "Nothing," she amended quickly.

His eyes narrowed. "You see right inside people, don't you?"

The flush grew deeper, making her look pretty. It irritated him. He'd had enough of women for the time being, even as acquaintances.

"Don't let Hartman railroad you into anything," he said out of the blue. "He's pushy, and he won't stop until he gets a story, if he's after one. Don't share anything you don't want the whole planet to see."

She laughed. "I'd already figured that out," she said softly. "He's like a bulldozer."

"I know."

"Yes, because you're like that," she blurted out, "except you don't do it for material gain . . ." She ground her teeth together and looked away from his shocked, angry face. "I'm sorry," she bit off. "That just slipped out. I'm really sorry," she repeated, her eyes pleading.

He took a deep breath. "You take some getting used to," he muttered.

"I don't do it on purpose," she told him quietly. "It's just something I was born with. I know things. I don't know how."

His dark eyes narrowed on her face. "Do your people come from Scotland originally?"

She caught her breath. How had he known that?! "Well, yes. On both sides of my family."

"Any McLeods or Stewarts in your lineage?" he persisted.

She was shell-shocked. "Yes. Both."

He smiled softly. "Both were known for having the 'second sight.'"

"Really?" she exclaimed. This was exciting.

"Really." He reached for his cup and saucer. She dived for her own. They both got up. "Next time you need a ride to Denver, let me know. I'll tell you about the clans on the way up."

"Oh, there's a party next weekend. Mr. Hartman said he'd come get me . . ." She frowned.

"I'll pass along your regrets to Mr. Hartman and I'll drive you up."

"But it's a party . . ."

"I was invited, too," he said, and smiled.

She laughed and flushed a little, because it was flattering that he'd volunteered to take her.

"Just one thing," he said, and he became serious.

"Yes, it's just a casual thing so don't start weaving daydreams around you," she finished for him, with humor sparkling in her silver eyes.

"Damn," he bit off.

"Sorry. Ancestry," she added, warding him off.

He rolled his eyes as they started for the counter. When they got to it, he snatched her bill out of her hand and paid for both.

She protested all the way out of the coffee shop.

"Next time, it's your treat," he said simply.

She hesitated. That sounded fair. "Okay." She nodded.

He smiled. He liked the way she only came up to his shoulder. She was pert and perky and smart and cute. Of course, there was that odd perception in her. But she was unlikely to guess certain things about him, and nobody alive knew them. It was safe enough to escort her to a party in Denver, he assured himself. He wasn't getting involved.

"Cell phone?" he asked, holding out his hand.

She was surprised into handing it over. He made a face as he opened her contacts list and put his number there, obtaining hers at the same time. "Good Lord," he muttered. "Why don't you go and buy a decent phone? Surely you can afford one now."

She gasped. "Do you know everything?" she asked, aghast.

"Why not? You do," he accused, but this time his dark eyes were sparkling.

She laughed. "Okay."

"I'll phone you when I'm on the way Saturday," he said. He eyed her. "Buy something silver," he said abruptly. "It will suit you. See you," he added, and he was gone, just that quickly.

One of the girls who worked as a clerk in the sheriff's office was coming toward her. Tess Lowery went to the same church as Sara. They'd known each other for years.

Tess stopped, grinning. "That is the first time I've ever seen Ty Blakeney take a woman into a coffee shop. Barring that barracuda he used to be mixed up with," she added, with rolling eyes. "She was as cold as ice. No feelings at all. None of us understood why a man like that would even waste his time on her." She grinned. "Of course, we had a pretty good idea. Still, he's too nice for that sort of woman."

"We just had coffee," Sara protested. "He was warning me about a man in Denver who wants to do a story about me."

"The guy in the sports car?" The woman nodded. She made a face. "Danny Hartman. We know him even over here in Benton. He's bad news." She shook a finger at Sara. "You're a nice person. I've known you for years," she added. "Don't you let that awful radio man take you for a ride."

Sara laughed. "Tess, I wouldn't dare," she replied.

"Ty Blakeney's a much better bet. Under all that coldness, I'll bet there's a lava pit," she teased.

"He's just driving me to Denver is all," Sara protested. "He's warned me off twice already . . ."

"Really?!"

Sara glared at her. "You stop that," she muttered.

"I can't help it. My life is like a sports news item. Yours is more like an ongoing soap opera."

Sara shook her head. "Don't I know it!"

"How's your wuppie?" she asked.

Sara laughed. "He's just great until we leave him alone in the house."

"He just needs a babysitter," Tess advised.

"Babysitter! Oh, my gosh, I can't go to a party. I don't have anybody to stay with Ed . . . !"

"Call Mrs. Grimes," Tess suggested. "She doesn't charge much and she loves kids and dogs. And you know her from church," Tess added with a smile.

"You're a lifesaver!" Sara said. "And yes, I've known Mrs. Grimes for years!"

"Her number's in the phone book. And there's a sale at the Benton Boutique," Tess added. "Hint, hint. They even have evening bags and sexy high heels on sale."

"I'll go right now," Sara said.

"Who's staying with Ed?"

"He's at class."

Tess frowned. "Kindergarten?"

Sara laughed. "No. Art class. He's taking lessons from Mrs. Scott. She's so talented!"

"Yes, she is." Tess hesitated. "You're not teaching him?"

"He doesn't pay attention to me. Mrs. Scott is creative. She inspires him!"

"What about the wuppie?"

"We have a carpenter on speed dial," Sara advised, and they both laughed.

Sometimes, Sara thought, things fell into place with insane precision. She'd seen a beautiful silvery cocktail dress in the window of the little dress shop in Benton. It was high-necked, ankle-deep, with a swirling skirt and fitted waist. Sara was certain that they wouldn't have it in her size.

But the model was exactly her size, and it fit her like a glove. She pirouetted in front of the full-length mirror with wide eyes. It was perfect, and it did something witchy to her silvery eyes.

"That really suits you," the saleswoman said. "And it's amazing, because we've only got one, and you're wearing it."

"It was meant for me." Sara laughed.

"I'd second that," the other woman agreed. "Besides, we have a matching pair of strappy high heels and an evening purse, if you're interested."

"I'm really interested," Sara replied. "Besides that, I need a new pair of jeans, a couple of T-shirts, and some new boots." She indicated the worn ones on her feet, which had been soaked so many times that the toes almost curled. "Ranch work wears them out really fast!"

"We've got a good selection of boots," the woman told her. "Need a jacket?"

"In the worst way." Sara sighed. "I've patched this old denim one so many times that it looks like it belongs to a hobo."

The saleswoman laughed.

"Do you have another denim one?"

"Let me look."

Sara took off the pretty dress and got back into her working clothes. She brought the dress out carefully on its hanger while the saleslady came back with a selection of jackets.

One of them was a newer and heavier denim jacket that reached to Sara's hips and had plenty of pockets.

"This one's just my style," Sara told her. "You can just never have too many pockets when you're working around livestock."

"Isn't it the truth?" the saleswoman agreed.

"Okay, I found two pairs of jeans and two T-shirts, and a couple of dresses for church. Now I need an evening purse and those strappy silver high heels," Sara replied.

"Right this way!"

Sara picked Ed up at his art class, after admiring his latest project, an impression of Goose that he'd drawn to the best of his young ability.

"It doesn't really look like him, does it?" he asked

sadly when they were getting out of the truck at the local department store, where Sara was taking him to get some new clothes.

"I think it's great," Sara told him with a warm smile. "It's not how accurate a drawing is, it's how much feeling you put into it. Drawing is like math; the more you do it, the better you get."

"Oh." Ed grinned.

"Now come on and let's get you some new clothes!"

"Can I have a T-shirt with a horse on it?" Ed asked.

"Sure you can."

They found him two T-shirts with horses, but Sara insisted on two plain ones to go with new jeans, and a new pair of sneakers. She also bought him a suit and some nice shoes to wear to church.

"Can't I just wear jeans to church?" he asked.

"Sure you could. But I always like to dress up for church. It's respectful, and it's not like we have any other place to be dressy," she replied.

"You're going up to the city to that party, though," Ed pointed out.

"Yes, I am, and Mrs. Grimes is going to babysit you and the wuppie," she said.

"Can't I go, too?" he asked plaintively.

She stopped and hugged him. "Any other time, yes, you could. But this is a big-people party," she said. "It's sort of like going to work." She wasn't sure about that, but it had seemed like it, when Danny Hartman had spoken to her about going.

"You can't go by yourself," Ed said.

"I'm not. Mr. Blakeney is going to drive me."

He nodded. "I like him."

She smiled. "I like him, too."

"I don't like Mr. Hartman," he added. "He's mean, like Daddy was when he was drinking. Except Mr. Hartman doesn't have to drink to be mean. He just is."

She wrinkled her forehead. "You're pretty keen, Ed."

"If he hurts you, I'll sic Goose on him. Goose didn't like him, either," Ed added.

"I noticed that."

"I'll bet he'd like Mr. Blakeney, though," Ed added.

Sara thought so, too, but she didn't say so.

They watched the news on their new color television, the night before the party in Denver.

"I like our new TV," Ed said, sprawled on the area rug in front of it.

"Me, too."

"But I like the Xbox best of all." He giggled.

Sara had splurged to buy it for him. One of the boys in his art class played on it, and he'd asked Ed if he had an Xbox. They could play together if Ed got one, he added.

Ed had gone without so much in his young life that Sara felt guilty. She bought him the game system and a couple of CDs for it. She surprised herself by enjoying the games as much as her little brother did. They already had the Internet connection to go online—Sara couldn't do without it on the ranch. But she did upgrade their conservative plan to a faster modem speed.

That Sara liked playing on the Xbox had amused Ed no end. There was a way to do a split screen and play against each other in the arcade game. Ed and Sara had enjoyed it so much that they rarely watched television anymore. Gaming was far more fun.

The night of the Denver party, Mrs. Grimes arrived just before Ty Blakeney did. Sara was all thumbs, nervous and jittery.

"Maybe I should just stay home," she told Ed and Mrs. Grimes.

"Nonsense." Mrs. Grimes chuckled. "Ed and I will have fun. And so will you, once you get there. You've never had much of a social life, Sara. It's about time you did."

"I'm not sure I'm cut out for a social life," Sara groaned.

"I know I'm not," Mrs. Grimes agreed. "So I stay home and play World of Warcraft and Destiny 2."

"What're those?" Ed asked, all eyes.

"World of Warcraft is a computer game," Mrs. Grimes told him, her blue eyes lighting up with pleasure. "I've played it for fifteen years. You can go on raids and do dungeons, and you can be a caster or a melee fighter. I play with people from all over the world. It's great fun!"

"And what's Destiny 2?" Ed persisted.

"That's an Xbox game," she said. She pulled a CD out of her purse and showed it to Ed. "I brought my copy over so we can play it!"

"Oh, boy!" Ed exclaimed. "It's got spaceships!"

"You've found the way to his heart." Sara chuckled.

"Do you play?" Mrs. Grimes asked her.

"In fact, I'm just learning to," Sara replied. "It's something Ed loves, and I like having something we can share."

"Well, this is one of the best . . ."

A sharp rap on the front door cut her off.

Sara went to open it. Ty Blakeney gave her a long look out of dark eyes, approving of the color and fit of the dress she was wearing.

"Not bad, Miss Whittaker," he murmured lazily. "You look very nice."

She was flustered and trying to hide it. "Thanks. You, too. Come on in."

He closed the door behind him and moved into the living room, where Ed was loading Destiny 2 into the Xbox.

"That's my favorite game," he remarked, nodding toward the television set where the Destiny logo was being displayed.

"Is it, really?" Mrs. Grimes asked. "Mine, too!"

He gaped at her. She was all of sixty, with silver hair and blue eyes and a warm smile.

"Well, I'm not too old to ride a rocket bike, you know," she told him.

He chuckled. "So much for my idea of what senior citizens do."

She wrinkled her nose. "We don't rock and knit anymore. Now it's two-handed swords and battlegrounds in World of Warcraft." She cocked her head. "In fact,

Horde wins more battlegrounds than Alliance on my server." She leaned forward with a wicked smile. "I'm Horde."

He pursed his lips. "So am I."

Sara, all at sea, had no idea what they were talking about.

"I'll explain it to you on the way to Denver," Ty told her. He glanced at his watch. "And we'd better go." He paused. "Where's the wuppie?" he added.

"Oh!" Ed got up and ran out of the room. He ran back in with a pretty little bundle of black-and-tan fur.

"Well!" Ty exclaimed.

Goose made a beeline toward him. He went down on one knee and ruffled the little animal's fur.

"You're a beaut, Goose," Ty said in a deep, soft tone while the puppy tried to get closer to him. He looked up. "Why 'Goose'?" he asked.

"In my book, it says a goose is fearless," Ed said.

"They are," Ty agreed. "They make good watch-dogs. Goose will protect both of you, when he gets a bit bigger. Does he play with toys?"

"Yes," Sara said. "He loves balls. Ed and I are teaching him to play fetch."

"He's going to be amazing," Ty replied, ruffling the puppy's fur one more time before he stood up. "We need to go," he told Sara.

"You two have fun. Ed and I will fight monsters," Mrs. Grimes said.

"Where's the other controller?" Sara asked Ed.

He looked sheepish. He drew it out from under the coffee table and handed it to Sara.

She groaned. It had teeth marks.

"He'll grow up," Ty told them, and chuckled. "Right now, he's exploring the world, and he does that with his mouth. Besides," he added, "a few teeth marks aren't going to affect the controller so much."

"I guess not," Sara said, shaking her head as she looked down at the panting, happy puppy.

"We won't be late," Ty told the others as he herded Sara out the door.

Chapter 4

"I've known Mrs. Grimes most of my life. I never knew she was a gamer," Sara said, laughing.

"It's a new world. My mother, God rest her soul, wouldn't have known a game controller from a TV controller."

She studied him quietly. "I wouldn't have taken you for a gamer."

"You'd be surprised at how many of us there are," he replied. "It's a help if you go into the military. The same sort of software used in gaming is used to control drones."

She nodded. "I've read about that."

He smiled. "I like your little brother," he said.

She smiled. "I like him, too."

"How did Hartman like Goose?" he asked abruptly.

"He doesn't like animals. Or much of anything else," she said shortly, her hands gripping her purse tightly.

He glanced at her and back at the road ahead. "He's never let sentiment get in the way of making more money," he said curtly.

"Money." She sighed, shaking her head. "I mean, it's

nice to be able to pay the bills and afford an occasional cup of fancy coffee or an ice cream cone. But you can't take it with you."

He smiled gently. "You're an odd person."

"I am?"

"I don't mean that in an insulting way," he said easily. "I don't think I've ever met anyone quite like you."

"I had a fraught childhood. I learned to duck and hide and run for my life early on," she added with a grin.

He laughed, as he was meant to. "Your father spent a lot of time getting wasted in bars. Do you know why?"

"He lost Mama and he couldn't go on," she said.

He gave her a long look as they stopped for a traffic light.

She narrowed her own eyes. "You know something that I don't," she guessed.

He nodded.

"Going to tell me?" she asked softly.

He hesitated.

"It can't be anything from my childhood," she said, thinking aloud. "So it has to be before I was born, right?"

She was quick-witted. He hadn't meant to say anything, but perhaps he should. She was carrying a lot of emotional scars because of her father.

"You almost had a brother before you were born," he said quietly. "Your father knew your mother was friendly with a former boyfriend, and he got it into his head that the child was the other man's."

"But Mama would have never . . . !" she began earnestly.

"Everybody except your father knew that," he continued. "Anyway, she was determined to prove her innocence so she had bloodwork done that would prove it." He concentrated on the road ahead. "The day the DNA profile came back. She lost the child."

"Oh, my gosh," she said, grimacing.

"They said he went mad when he had the evidence that cleared her. It was too late for the child, of course."

"What did Mama do?"

"Old man Wheeler said she came to him, hoping to buy a ticket back to Texas, where her people were. But your father followed her to town, in tears, and begged her to stay, apologizing literally on his knees." He glowered. "So she stayed. He was never vicious to her during any of her next two pregnancies, and Wheeler said he was over the moon when your little brother came along. He finally had his son."

"Yes. He wasn't particularly fond of me," she said philosophically, with a sad smile. "He thought girls were useless."

"But he thought about that first child, and Wheeler said it played on his mind that he'd caused the death. He started drinking more than ever. Sheriff Ralston and his deputies spent a lot of time at your house when you were a kid. He stayed sober for a while after your brother was born, but the boy only reminded him of the child he'd lost. His conscience tormented him. He took it out on all of you, even your little brother, at the last."

She sighed, leaning her head back against the seat. "I figured there had to be a reason for it. I just wish he'd had therapy. It might have helped all of us."

"He didn't believe in such things."

She laughed softly. "He didn't believe in anything, to hear him talk. But when he was dying, he prayed." Her eyes had a faraway look. "Faith was all I had during those years. My knees got a workout." She glanced at him. "Did you know my father?"

He smiled mysteriously. "Let's not open that can of worms tonight."

So there was something more, something he knew that he hadn't shared. She turned her purse over on her lap, fidgeting. She glanced at him. He was in his early thirties. Certainly he wasn't old enough to have known her father when she was a child.

"Busy little mind, spinning around looking for truth," he mused. "Careful. You might find it one day."

"It won't be for lack of trying." The purse stilled in her pretty hands. "You haven't lived here for a long time," she began, trying to put things together from vague clues.

"Nope," he agreed.

"You keep to yourself. No housekeeper, only a few cowboys to help you run the ranch, and they're old friends, everybody says. No strangers. No women, at all."

"I had a fiancée," he replied curtly. "She was jealous and violent with it. I kept women away from the place."

She wasn't sure if it was safe to ask him anything about the shadowy woman who had shattered his life. It had been several months, but townspeople said it was dangerous to ask him about her. She decided that her questions weren't important enough to take the chance.

She looked out the window instead.

He smiled, understanding her silence without saying it out loud. She wasn't a pushy sort of woman. She seemed content with her lot, although selling that painting had astonished her. She'd been practically giving away her work, with no real knowledge of its worth. Now she'd have some sort of financial security. She could have a life of her own. Although, the child would make that difficult. He frowned.

Children had been a sticking point with his vanished fiancée. He wanted them. She didn't. And it was a position she wouldn't even discuss.

He'd been almost suicidal after losing her. His agent had been ecstatic. He hadn't produced anything in months, because his fiancée was jealous of the computer. He'd thought about sharing his work with her, until she complained that people in the arts were just lazy layabouts with no ambition, and she'd never get mixed up with one.

It had shattered him. He was well-known in his field, and he'd grown wealthy from its pursuit. But the love of his life had no place in hers for a career-oriented man. So he'd pretended for those months that he was financially secure due to an inheritance, and kept the rest to himself. The computer probably had spiderwebs by now, he thought, and chuckled.

"What's funny?" she asked, diverted.

"Spiderwebs," he murmured.

She gave him a stunned look.

"I was picturing them on my computer," he said.

"Oh. The gaming one." She nodded, remembering what he'd said about his hobby.

"That's right," he replied. "The gaming one."

She frowned. "Didn't she like it when you played?"

"Not particularly," he said, and this time his deep voice had a bite in it.

"Sorry," she said softly. "I didn't mean to dig up bad memories."

He shifted behind the wheel. "I'm less touchy than I was," he said after a minute. He glanced at her and then back to the long road ahead. "Haven't you ever thought about a home of your own, a family? I know you love your brother, but there are good foster homes . . ."

"No."

Just the one word. But the inflection in it alluded to fire and brimstone if anybody tried to take away her baby brother.

"It will stunt your social life," he said. "Most men don't want to be part of a ready-made family."

"That's their loss," she said. "I promised myself when Mama died that I'd take care of Ed until he was grown, and that's what I'm going to do."

"How old are you?" he asked.

He'd forgotten. She'd told him before. She sighed. "Twenty-four."

"And he's, what, four? By the time he's in college you'll be thirty-four. That's a bit too late for a woman to get married and start a family."

"I might never marry," she said simply. "Lots of people don't."

He just shook his head.

"There's this thing called responsibility," she said quietly. "It's not talked about much, because it's easier to pass the buck, to blame somebody or something else if you mess up. I'm old-fashioned enough to believe in it. That, and accountability, and purpose." She turned in her seat. "Do you ever watch Congress on C-Span?" she asked.

He grimaced. "I try not to."

"Yes, because every person who's brought before it has the same excuse. I was just doing my job. I failed because such and such other person failed. What I said was taken out of context. That's not what I meant. I don't have that information right now." She rolled her eyes. "They talk in circles. You can't get one single person who heads any government agency to answer a question. They answer a question that wasn't even asked, or they stonewall. The kindest thing that could happen to this country would be if one of those unidentified flying objects came down, sucked up every politician in D.C., and carried them off to some other planet!"

He was roaring with laughter.

"Well, it's the truth," she said, calming down.

"Yes, it is," he agreed. He pulled into a long driveway. "But you'd better keep those thoughts to yourself just for this evening." He stopped the truck under an archway of a huge, lighted mansion, got out, helped her out, and tossed the keys to one of the valets.

"Why do I need to keep it to myself?" she asked, as they walked up the wide steps.

"Because the senior senator from Colorado lives

here," he whispered into her ear, and chuckled when she started and almost tripped.

He escorted her into the luxurious dining room, where trays of canapés were being placed on long tables, sharing space with champagne and hard liquor and crystal glasses.

"Wow," she murmured. "This is a far cry from a McDonald's coke with a straw in a paper cup."

"It's another world," he agreed, handing her a glass of champagne.

"I don't drink," she said, trying to put the glass down.

"I'm driving. It's just for one night, to be sociable. Keep it."

She sighed, and took a sip. She wrinkled her nose. "It tickles."

"The more you drink, the less it tickles," he assured her.

She shrugged, and took another sip.

Their hosts from the previous party in Denver were also guests here. They came to renew acquaintances.

"Ty, it's so nice to see you out again," the wife of the gallery owner said, smiling. "Twice, in one month, too." She leaned closer. "Don't tell me you're dusting spiderwebs off the computer, too?"

He laughed. "I guess I am."

"About time!" she told him. "Everybody's looking forward to the sequel."

He put his finger to his lips while Sara wasn't looking.

The other woman caught on quickly. She grinned and nodded.

About that time, Danny Hartman spotted them and made a beeline for Sara. Out of some ancient darkness, Ty recalled why Danny had no business trying to take over Sara's life. He reached down for her hand and slowly locked his fingers into hers.

Her small hand jerked faintly at the unfamiliar touch. Her breath caught. Her heart ran wild. She tried valiantly to stop her involuntary reaction to him. He was very attractive, and just being with him made her happy.

Warning bells went off in her head. She looked up at him. "Is this some reverse psychology sort of thing?" she asked in a whisper.

He blinked. "A what?" he asked.

"Well, you told me not to weave daydreams about you," she said. She indicated their linked hands. "You shouldn't encourage me."

He chuckled. She was a constant delight. He hadn't had any joy in his life for so long. He'd almost forgotten how to laugh.

"And no fair making fun of your admirers," she added. "Heavens, I might push you down on the floor and kiss you to death! You don't know!"

He was almost bursting now.

Danny Hartman walked up, frowning. Blakeney had refused a ride for her to the gallery. Hartman had hoped to have her to himself so that he could pry into her life and seduce her, as he'd seduced many other women— including Blakeney's promiscuous former girlfriend. But apparently Sara was now in his nemesis's crosshairs.

He wondered how much she knew about the man holding her hand. He was dangerous. Hartman left him strictly alone, despite the fact that even one chapter of Blakeney's life would outsell anything Hartman had ever published. He'd tried and failed a few years back to do a story about the man beside Sara.

He'd carefully approached the chief editor about doing an article on Blakeney. He was given a go-ahead, but a single phone call from D.C. had caused the editor to stop Hartman in his tracks. He was told never to ask questions about Blakeney. The consequences could be dire.

So Hartman left the enigmatic author strictly alone except for occasional sarcastic digs at parties. Even then, there was a red line. Nobody sane crossed it. Blakeney's books were full of espionage and firefights. They referenced subjects rarely discussed outside spec ops teams. Which led Hartman to ponder how Blakeney obtained that information. It would take a high-security clearance and probably permission from some shadow agency to even be able to refer to it in a work of fiction.

Whatever Blakeney knew had made him a bestselling author, published all over the world. He went from being the owner of a broken-down ranch to a man who could pay cash for a Rolls-Royce.

Hartman hated him for that. He had talent. He wrote for a major news organization. That should have been him making that sort of money, not Blakeney, who was more a recluse than a party goer.

"Thanks for bringing my girl up for the party."

Hartman threw down the gauntlet, ignoring those locked hands.

"I'm not your girl, Mr. Hartman," Sara said, smiling blithely. "As you can see"—she held up her clasped fingers—"I'm doing my best to worm my way into Mr. Blakeney's heart. Please don't interrupt me."

Blakeney burst out laughing, which made Hartman even more furious. His face grew red with temper.

"You won't be laughing when I finish my investigation," Hartman told the other man with narrowed eyes.

Blakeney just shrugged. "You're welcome to investigate all you like," he told Hartman. He even smiled. "Until you hit the stone wall ahead of you at top speed."

"How do you get all that information?" he wanted to know. "My contact says you have a higher security clearance than some members of Congress!"

Blakeney cocked his head and just stared at the other man. "There are many levels of classification," he said patiently. "But it's not what you know. It's who you know."

"I'll find out," Hartman threatened.

"You won't," was the firm reply. "And if you dig deep enough," he added in a soft, deep undertone, "you'll bury yourself."

"Is that a threat?"

"It's a fact," Blakeney replied. He looked over Hartman's shoulder at Senator John Hughes, a tall silver-haired man with great dignity, who was coming toward them. "But don't take my word for it. Ask John," he added, smiling at the senator as he approached.

"Well, damn, are you still alive?" John Hughes laughed,

shaking hands with Blakeney, who still had his left hand tightly entangled with Sara's.

"Still alive and kicking." Blakeney chuckled.

"Hartman, isn't it?" Hughes added, and his tone changed as he faced the reporter. His eyes narrowed. "You and I will never see eye to eye on any political issues. I didn't appreciate your slanted piece on the legislation I suggested to the House committee last month."

"It was hardly slanted . . ." Hartman began defensively.

"It was slanted so far that even my worst colleague said it was overdone," he interrupted. "Journalism involves fair play. You tell both sides of the issue, not just the one you prefer, and you let the public decide. You don't get behind people and push them toward your point of view."

"My editor . . ." Hartman began again.

"Your editor is lining up for an investigative committee hearing," was the senator's reply. He smiled coldly. "I have that from the highest authority. You have permission to pass it along. You might add that I'm quite aware of his shadow dealing, and he's already attracted the attention of the one agency you don't want coming up behind you in a dark alley. He's passed a red line. A very red line."

Hartman's heart was racing. He and the editor both had invested in what sounded like a sure thing, even though it was just past the limit on legal activities. They both knew how their investments were handled farther down the line. They knew how deadly their colleagues were. They thought that, because they were so deadly, no politician would dare stick his nose into an investigation.

But he knew which agency the senator was referring to, and it struck him like a lightning bolt. If it came out publicly, his paper would lose subscribers and he would lose his job, if not his freedom. The publisher, who rarely stuck his nose into the businesses he owned, had no idea what his chief editor and his chief reporter were dabbling in. Even less did he know that their illegal dealings could land all of them in prison.

Hartman felt his feet go cold as he contemplated what Senator Hughes was saying.

"You can tell your editor that he'd better back out of any upcoming deals and find legal counsel." He leaned forward. "That goes for you, too, Hartman. All the deals being made undercover are being brought out by citizen journalists on the Internet. You can't hide anymore. People are tired of unpunished crime. The penalties in the future will make this decade look like an amusement park for crime. If I were you," he added, "I'd pull my neck back while there was still time."

Blakeney hadn't said a word. The hand holding Sara's was warm and strong and firm. It gave her a feeling of utter security, shelter in the storms of life. And even while she was feeling that, she knew that this man was more eagle than songbird. He wouldn't be nesting in some safe tree. He'd be out hunting, free and unfettered by emotional ties.

It was just that the feelings she had were new and exciting. Her life so far had been one of service and sacrifice. She'd had no time or opportunity for any romance in her sad life. It made sense that she'd go giddy the first time a man, an attractive man, came close to her. But she had to force down these emotions. They were unwelcome and not just to her. She could absolutely feel the tension in the man next to her. He was hating this pretense.

Actually, he was feeling the same things Sara was. Comfort. Security. Compassion. All those things, and more. He had a rough past that he was still dealing with, ten years after the fact. People whose lives had brushed his at any point were a painful reminder of things he'd done, things he'd seen.

He'd had a brief round of psychological help, after the fact. But the therapist hadn't been able to get him to open up about his past. He shared it with nobody, least of all his former girlfriend who'd abandoned him for somebody richer. Actually, the joke was on her, because now he had more assets than her new paramour. She'd abandoned him too quickly.

Amusedly, she'd tried to get him back the week before. She'd called and complained that her new boyfriend neglected her and she was so lonely. Wouldn't he like for her to come back and visit? He'd laughed, told her sorry, he was through with that part of his life.

She'd slung insults at him. He hung up in the middle of them and didn't even feel regret. It was that day that he'd had coffee with Sara in the coffee shop in Benton. He smiled to himself at the memory. He'd been a little morose after the conversation as he remembered good times with his former girlfriend. But Sara, level-headed

Sara, had dug out the pain and replaced it with simple compassion.

He looked down at her. She was striking in the silver dress that matched her pale eyes. The contrast with her dark, wavy hair was also striking. She wasn't beautiful but she had a warmth that embraced everybody she came close to. People responded to her. It was a gift, like her ability to see inside people. He'd never known anyone like her. And he didn't like the feelings she aroused in him. But he couldn't abandon her to Danny Hartman. The man was brutal. Blakeney knew things about him that Sara wouldn't have dreamed. He couldn't share them without revealing his own past. But he wasn't going to let Hartman one step closer.

Hartman was fuming. He'd been checkmated without making a single move. He glared at the senator, who was still listing his grievances. But the veiled threat from Blakeney affected him much more. He thought the activities of the men he and his editor backed were unknown to polite society. Now he knew differently. And he didn't know what to do. For the first time in his life, he was frightened.

Blakeney saw that panic and understood it. His hand held Sara's more securely and drew her just a little closer.

She looked up at him with faint surprise.

He met that wide-eyed stare with an unsmiling one. His heart was beating double time. He stared into her pale silver eyes and felt the reaction go through him like a blow.

There were places inside him that no one had ever seen, places he kept hidden from everyone. But Sara looked at him and he could see himself through her eyes, see the soft interest, the warmth, the comfort that he'd been seeking all his life. What a strange place to find it, in a young woman he barely knew. But then, he'd known her forever. It felt like that when he was around her. As if there were no secrets that they hadn't shared.

He had beautiful eyes, she thought as she stared into them. He was beautiful, in a rough-hewn sort of way. He was the end result of all the tragedies of his life. He thought they were hidden, but he bore the scars. Sara didn't have to see them to know they were there.

She understood, because she'd gone through the wars in her own way, with her brutal parent.

"Ty!"

He started at the sound of his name.

The senator chuckled; he could see the attraction between his friend and this young lady. He expected that Ty would fight it to the death. The man was a loner if there ever was one. Or, at least, he had been before that spider of a woman got her claws into him. What luck that she found another sucker before she destroyed Ty's life. She'd already cost him months out of publication, which was deadly even for a top-ranked author. The public forgot quickly when the books stopped coming, and they found other authors to fill the gap. Ty was well rid of her.

"I said, I have to leave early. I've got to get back to D.C. tonight," John told Ty. He shook hands. "Try to stay out of trouble."

"I never get in trouble," Ty said with a grin.

"Any day now . . . ." Hartman grumbled with a glare.

"I was about to say the same thing to you, Hartman," Ty said with a faint smile.

"Don't forget what I told you," Hughes told Hartman, and he wasn't smiling. "You and your editor are under the magnifying glass. You're being watched." Hartman went pale as Hughes turned back to Ty. "I'll be in touch," he promised.

Ty chuckled. "It won't help."

"One day you'll agree," the senator assured him.

Ty shook his head. "Not my thing," he said. "Not anymore."

"Oh, that's rich," Hartman said coldly. "Isn't that what you said last time . . . ?"

"Just before your little hit piece came out, you mean?" Ty asked him. One eyebrow lifted. "I was going to say no. But this time there were children involved," he added coldly. "And you know exactly what I mean."

Hartman swallowed. Hard. "I . . . I do not," he faltered.

"You'd better hope for a friendly journalist to cover what's coming up," Ty told him. "Or you'll be fried like a big fish, on the same grill with your idiot editor."

Sara was staring at Hartman, as if she saw something that puzzled her. And, in fact, she was puzzled.

"You didn't care where the money came from," she said, as if in a trance. "But then you don't know what happened to the children who were taken away from their families when they reached the sanctuary. And you didn't care. But you will," she added softly. She grimaced. "I'm sorry for you."

Hartman was offended. "Be sorry for yourself, getting mixed up with him," he said, indicating Ty. "Nothing

I've ever done is half as bad as the things he's been accused of. And he's so protected that he never gets called out for it!"

"That's enough," Ty said. His whole demeanor changed. He went from placid conversation to quiet fury in seconds, all without raising his voice or moving a muscle. But Hartman actually backed up a step.

He turned away. "If you'll excuse me, I have important people to talk to." He didn't look at them as he made his way through the crowd to the drinks table.

Sara moved closer to Ty, so close that she could feel the heat and strength of his fit body. He smelled of soap and spices. Her hand in his became quietly caressing. "It's all right," she said softly.

He was so enraged that his body felt like iron. But as he looked down into Sara's soft face, his anger seemed to flow down through his shoes into the floor. He took a breath and it was like coming up out of tremendous depths.

"What?" he asked, going blank for a few seconds, with painful memories.

"It's all right," she repeated.

"You don't know what you're talking about," he said icily.

Her pale eyes searched his strong, taut face. "Yes, I do," she replied. "War invites all sort of tragedies. It enables actions that are illegal but necessary to save lives." She reached up with her free hand and touched his chin. "You aren't the only one who came home with nightmares," she added in a slow, tender voice.

"Blaming yourself for things you can't control, that's not sensible."

He took another breath and slowly shook his head. "How do you do that?" he asked softly.

"Do what?"

He linked their hands closer and turned toward her. "Face a charging bear and turn it into a stuffed animal," he mused, smiling.

She shrugged. "Sometimes it doesn't work," she said, and pain was in her beautiful eyes as she recalled trying to talk her father down from a drunken rage.

He winced, because he could almost see it through her eyes. "Long years of practice," he murmured.

She nodded. She took a breath and smiled. "Life hurts," she said simply.

He smiled back. He just nodded.

They left while the party was still going on. Sara made two new contacts in the art gallery owners who attended, and she promised canvases if they could send her photographs of the people they wanted her to portray.

"Heavens, I'll have to learn to paint with both hands as well as both feet," she exclaimed on the way home. "How could I be so stupid? I'll never get caught up!"

He just laughed. "You'll find a way."

She leaned back and stretched. "I can try." She laid her head back against the seat and looked at him while he drove. "You and Danny Hartman have a past."

Her perceptions didn't disturb him so much anymore. "Yes," he said simply.

"He's doing some really terrible things," she remarked.

"Worse than you know. And the ax is about to fall."

"Good. A better neck would be hard to find," she muttered.

He burst out laughing.

"I mean it," she insisted. "I thought he was such a nice man. He wanted to do a story about me. He wanted to help me find buyers for my art. He even offered to come all this way and drive me to that party in Denver." She grimaced. "I finally saw through him. I'm glad I ran into you at the coffee shop. You saved me."

He'd saved her from more than she knew. And he hadn't run into her by accident. He knew a lot about Danny Hartman. Too much to abandon her to his predatory stalking.

"Thanks," she said.

"Don't mention it," he replied. "Next time, you can save me."

She laughed. "From what?"

"Predatory females?"

She smiled. "Found a lot of those, have we?"

He glanced at her amused expression. She didn't know him yet. She wasn't aware that he had a huge reader base, along with female fans who had actively pursued him in the past.

Of course, he'd been out of circulation for a year. He frowned. He had to do something about that. He'd go fishing tomorrow, he thought. The weather was unseasonably warm and he knew a good spot to just sit and think. He had several ideas whirling around in his head. He'd have to grab a few and put them together.

"What are you thinking about so hard?" she wondered.

"Fishing."

She laughed.

"No, really. I like fishing."

She nodded. "Me, too. I used to go to the river with my grandad and fish for trout. That was years ago."

"Trout fishing is fun. And even though it's barely March, despite the recent snow, there's rainbow and brown trout in the rivers."

She grinned. "Grandad didn't think it was fun. I caught three trout. He caught an old boot."

He chuckled. "Poor old man."

"Yes, I know. It wasn't even his size!"

He shook his head. He couldn't remember ever having such fun with a woman.

Sara was thinking the same thing about him. She'd been afraid of men for a long time. But this one, even when he was furious, was calm and quiet. She wasn't afraid of him. Not at all. Her eyes moved over his face like exploring fingers.

"Don't," he cautioned.

"What?"

"Don't start daydreaming about me."

"Well, darn," she muttered. "Who else am I going to daydream about? And if you say Danny Hartman, I'll hit you with a dead fish."

"Where will you get one?"

"I'll fish one up and bring it to you," she said. "Then I'll hit you with it."

"Might take some time."

"I'm in no rush," she countered.

"In that case, you can go fishing with me tomorrow. Is Ed in school yet?"

"No, but he has a drawing class in the morning from nine 'til noon."

"I'll pick you both up at a quarter to nine. We can drop Ed off on the way. What about puppy dog?"

"The wuppie?" she teased, all alight about the fishing trip. "I'll get a babysitter."

He chuckled. "Got it all worked out already?"

"You bet! I haven't been fishing in years!" She grimaced. "Oh, no!"

"What?"

"I don't have a rod and reel," she groaned.

"I've got half a dozen. You can take your pick," he said.

"In that case, I'll be ready to go on time. Ed, too." She hesitated. "Thanks."

"For what? Sticking you on a riverbank with stinging insects?"

"For asking me to go," she said. "I haven't been anywhere except home and work for . . . for a really long time, except for two parties in Denver."

He felt those words keenly, but he didn't let on. He smiled blandly. "No problem. Fishing helps me solve problems sometimes."

She nodded. "Me, too." She didn't add that he was likely to become her biggest problem. He didn't want her daydreaming about him. But it was getting to the point that he was all she did daydream about. She was headed for tragedy and she knew it. But she couldn't help herself. Not at all.

CHAPTER 5

Ty pulled up at the front door of Sara's house. "Sit tight," he said when she started to open her door.

She was surprised, but she settled back into her seat. He opened the door, flicked off her seat belt, and pulled her out of the truck, holding her cradled in his arms.

Her heart went wild. She managed to catch her breath, if only slightly. Her arms twined around his neck.

"This is a very bad idea," she said softly.

"Is it? Why?" he asked, searching her eyes in the light of the porch.

"I might get fixated on you," she said.

"Only happens to baby chicks and ducks," he said.

"Also happens to lonely spinsters who live out in the sticks," she said. "And don't ever say that I didn't warn . . . oh!"

While she was in full spate, he cut her off very gently by settling his hard, warm mouth over her own.

Oh, glory, she was thinking, as some incredible hunger suddenly sprouted up in her like a fountain out of nowhere. Her body was shaken into full, passionate life as the kiss slowly hardened and deepened, until she let out a helpless little sob as the feelings overwhelmed her.

He lifted his head just a breath away. "What was that all about?" he whispered.

"Escaping swamp gas," she breathed. "Local phenomenon. Ignore it."

He smiled. His mouth came down on hers again. And she ignored everything for long, sweet, mad seconds while he devoured her soft lips.

Finally, he was able to lift away from the sweetest hunger he'd ever felt. "You were right," he said on a heavy breath as he headed toward the front porch.

She was still winding in space mentally. "About what?"

"It was a bad idea," he said shortly, and helped her up onto the porch.

She looked up at him. "Maybe it was, but you can't back out."

He blinked. "Back out?"

"Fishing in the morning," she said. "Kissing people is no excuse for depriving people of fishing trips."

He cocked his head. His dark eyes were twinkling. "If you say so."

"Besides, I've spent whole minutes planning my wardrobe."

"To go fishing." He was looking at her with a strange expression.

"Exactly. I'm glad that you understand how important it is to choose just the right clothes for every occasion."

He eyed her lovely figure in the silver dress, where

her new coat had come undone. "Ha! You'd have bought a black dress if I hadn't told you to get a silver one."

She would have. She glared at him. "A momentary lapse," she said.

"We'll see about that." He turned and walked back toward the truck.

"If you're not here, I'll go by myself," she called after him. "All alone. In the wilds. Where there are bears!" She was raising her voice with every sentence. "I could be eaten!"

"Better be ready on time, then," he said. He got into the truck and left without another word.

She went into the house, where Ed and Mrs. Grimes were furiously battling each other on the screen. Puppy dog was lying on his back near the TV, sound asleep.

"I'm home," she said.

"Watch that beast coming out of the sand to your left, Ed. You'll get us eaten!"

"Okay, but you have to get the fat Mars guys on the right!" he exclaimed.

"Got it!"

There was furious gunfire of a science fiction sort.

Sara sighed, put her purse down, and went to change clothes. Laser rifle fire was still coming out of the living room ten minutes later.

"That was a super fight!" Ed said.

Two voices from the television agreed. So did Mrs. Grimes. They all said good night and Ed turned off the TV.

"You're great, Mrs. Grimes!" he exclaimed.

She hugged him. "And you're fantastic! Same time tomorrow night?"

"Same time! I'll tell the others. We'll raid!"

"Absolutely. Oh, hello, Sara! Did you have a good time?"

"It was really nice." She smiled. "I'm going fishing with him in the morning."

Mrs. Grimes stared at her. "Going fishing?"

"With Mr. Blakeney?" Ed chimed in.

"I have to."

"You have to?" Ed said.

She nodded solemnly. "I promised to hit him with a dead fish for something he said. I have to catch one first to make it dead. So I can hit him."

"What did he say?" Mrs. Grimes asked, retrieving her keys from her purse.

"I forget," she said. "But in case I remember, I really need to catch a fish. Ed, bedtime."

"Okay, sis." He hugged her. "Good night."

She kissed the top of his head. "You too, sport. Night night."

"Love you!" he called back.

"Love you, too!" she replied.

Mrs. Grimes smiled at the interaction. "You really love that boy, don't you?"

"With all my heart," she agreed, smiling softly.

"And our Mr. Blakeney, who's never seen with a female person these days, is taking you fishing. It must be the end of the world."

She laughed. "We had a good time at the party."

Mrs. Grimes looked at her with sad eyes: "Just don't

go in headfirst, okay? There are things about him that most people don't know."

"It won't matter," she said softly.

"I was afraid of that. Well, I have a broad shoulder. If you ever need one."

Sara smiled. "I know. And thank you so much." She stuffed a bill into the older woman's pocket and restrained her arm when she went to pull it out. "You know very well that I can afford it now. I won't let you put me under obligations," she added with wiggling eyebrows and a grin.

Mrs. Grimes laughed. "All right, then. Thank you. I'll buy more dog food for my Bennie."

"Was the wuppie okay?"

"Goose came in and watched us play and just went to sleep," she said. "I'll never understand puppies."

"Neither will I. Kitchen floor is okay, then?"

"It hasn't yet recovered from his last foray, after its first makeover," she replied. "I'd just wait until he's a couple of months older. No sense fixing it and have him tear it right back up for a second time if he gets mad at you, now, is there?"

"No sense at all. Thanks for taking care of my baby brother."

"Oh, I enjoyed it. We formed a raid group and had a ball shooting aliens with futuristic weapons!"

"I'm just looking forward to a long, sound sleep. Ed has a drawing class from nine to twelve, but can you come in the morning a little before nine to babysit the shredder?" she added.

Mrs. Grimes laughed. "Sure, I can."

"Okay, then. Thanks again. I'll see you in the morning."

Mrs. Grimes waved as she went out the door. "I'll be here at nine."

"Good night."

"Good night."

Sara locked up, turned out the lights in the other rooms, and went to bed. Goose had followed Ed back to his room and was already asleep at the side of the bed. Ed was asleep as well. She smiled as she closed the door.

Mrs. Grimes had mentioned secrets in Ty's past. She had a good idea what some of them were. She also remembered what Mrs. Grimes had said about Ty's inability to settle down. It was true. He was very much a free spirit.

But could a man kiss a woman the way he'd kissed her, and feel nothing? It seemed impossible. Then, again, what did she really know about men? Her first real date had been with Ty.

She turned out the lights and put all her worries in the back of her mind. She wasn't going to wrestle with the problem tonight. She was still floating on the cloud of sweet discovery.

Sara took Ed early to his drawing class. It was a peach of a day, unseasonably warm and the sun was out. It boded well for a fun activity. When she got back home, Mrs. Grimes had already arrived. She loaded up the game while Sara went to change clothes.

Sara came out wearing old jeans with worn places on

the knees. Under her flannel overshirt was a T-shirt with a subdued steampunk portrait. On her feet were boots with curled toes. She had on no makeup and her hair, always wavy and unruly, was mussed.

"Well?" she asked during a lull in laser cannon fire.

Mrs. Grimes blinked. "You're going like that?" she asked, surprised.

"It's a fishing trip. Mud. Smelly fish. Worms. We're unlikely to come across a fashion reporter," she replied with twinkling silver eyes.

"Good point," the older woman agreed. "How about lunch? You going out for it?"

"Not smelling like dead fish," Sara replied on a chuckle. "I packed Moon Pies and cans of Vienna sausages and crackers and cheese and soda."

"Should take a thermos of coffee, just in case you need propping up after the long periods of acute boredom." The other woman laughed.

"Good point. I'll make a pot and dig out two thermoses. I'd bet real money that Mr. Blakeney drinks his strong and black."

"Definitely."

"What do you know about him that I don't?" Sara asked. "And why?"

"I'm friends with a man who has contacts in some strange places. And that's all I'm telling you," Mrs. Grimes related. "So give it up. I won't talk. You might ask Blakeney."

"Not without a head start," Sara replied. "I don't expect he takes kindly to interrogation."

"That's a definite no," Mrs. Grimes said. "The last

guy who tried it needed dental work. He pushed just a little too hard."

"Who was he?" Sara asked curiously.

"A reporter for one of those strictly male magazines. He left town rather quickly."

"Our Mr. Blakeney has definite ideas about what he wants to tell people. I've noticed that."

Mrs. Grimes nodded. She got down two thermoses while Sara made strong coffee.

"Want to pack some creamer and sweetener?"

She shook her head. "I'd bet money that neither of us would ever use it."

"How did things work out with Mr. Hartman last night?" she asked.

Sara rolled her eyes. "It was educational. The two of them are like mountain goats in combat. Born enemies."

"Hartman has a bad reputation, even here," Mrs. Grimes said. "He's always looking for dirt that he can use in his column. He pushes people so that he can get them to confess things."

"It wouldn't work on Mr. Blakeney. He was angry. You could tell. But he never raised his voice or even drew back his fist."

"He has remarkable self-control. Our sheriff says he's never known anybody as cool under fire."

"Does Jeff know him?"

"Yes. They served together overseas in the Middle East."

"Army?"

"Jeff was in the army."

Sara turned. "And Mr. Blakeney?"

She just smiled.

"You're no help at all," Sara teased.

"I like having a future to look forward to."

"You're kidding."

"I'm not," Mrs. Grimes replied. "People have gone permanently missing for what I've already said."

Sara whistled.

"There's a big black budget in Washington. People will do anything to protect it. There's no oversight, no accountability. Power is involved. A lot of it. Nobody wants their boat rocked."

"I'm getting undertones of guys with big cigars and hidden automatic pistols."

"Good. Keep seeing those. It will keep you out of trouble."

"You mean, there really are . . . ?"

"I mean, keep in mind that certain factions operate that way. A lot of life is hidden under the cover of respectability. A very dirty sort."

"Mrs. Grimes, I think you must hang out with some very odd people," Sara accused as she filled the thermoses with black coffee.

The older woman chuckled. "I have a background that I don't share. I wasn't always a kindly old babysitter in a small Colorado town."

Sara turned and stared at her.

Mrs. Grimes just grinned.

Sara sighed. "I must live a sheltered life."

"You do. Let's keep it that way. And do I hear a truck driving up?"

Sara's heart jumped and she almost dropped the thermos.

Mrs. Grimes looked at her and laughed under her breath. "I'll go let him in."

"Do I look okay?" Sara asked quickly, flushed and flustered.

"Now isn't that a question you should have asked fifteen minutes ago?" she teased.

Sara glowered at her. "Spoilsport."

"You look like a woman on her way to a fishing hole," came the droll reply.

There was a quick rap at the back door and there he was, six feet of understated muscle in jeans and a blue flannel shirt and boots, with dark, sparkling eyes in a handsome, if unconventionally so, face.

"Come on in. Sara's just filling two thermoses."

"With black coffee, I hope," he said, stifling a yawn. "I was up working late."

Sara, who knew he had a ranch, assumed he was up with pregnant cows. They had a few here on her own ranch. They had to be carefully tended to give birth in the spring, and it wouldn't be long now until they were delivering.

"Yes, it's black coffee and very strong," Sara said, laughing. "Would you rather have a cup here first?"

He shook his head. "The air outside is just nippy enough to be pleasant. It will keep me awake. I have doughnuts in the truck," he added. "Freshly baked."

"Where did you get doughnuts this early?" she asked, surprised.

"Stole them from Jeff at the sheriff's department."

He chuckled. "He had a whole box and I lifted a couple while his back was turned."

"You stole doughnuts in the sheriff's office?" she exclaimed in mock horror.

"His secretary abetted me."

"You'll serve time," she promised.

"Nah. Community service, if anything. I'll volunteer to clean up his desk and he'll cut me loose in five minutes flat."

Sara, who'd seen the sheriff's desk, just laughed. "Probably," she agreed. She was trying not to look at him and failing miserably. Her heart was racing like a mad thing.

He checked his watch. "We should go," he said. "Before any other fishermen discover my spot."

"You can tell them we saw a Bigfoot and send them off searching for it," she advised.

"Not when trout are running." He chuckled. "Let's go."

"Have fun," Mrs. Grimes said. "I'll keep puppy dog out of trouble."

"Hello, Goose," Blakeney said, kneeling to pet the laughing puppy. "You're going to grow up to be a Clydesdale," he noted. "Paws like a Yeti!"

"The vet says he'll go one hundred pounds, easy," Sara replied. "He really is beautiful. Such a far cry from the bedraggled little thing Ed found on the side of the road."

"That seems like a hundred years ago," Blakeney remarked quietly. He was silent for a minute, still stroking the puppy, with a faraway look in his eyes. He got to his feet abruptly. "Let's get moving."

* * *

He was withdrawn all the way to the river. Sara glanced at him covertly, but she didn't ask questions. He was obviously working on a problem in his mind, because his concentration was absolute. He pulled up in a grove of trees beside a dirt path that led down to the river. Even though it was early, there were still fishermen around, many wearing hip boots.

She paused to watch them cast while Blakeney got the fishing poles and tackle out of the truck, along with a cooler for any fish they caught.

"That's a very small cooler," she noted.

His eyebrows arched under his wide-brimmed hat. "You planning on landing something upward of ten pounds?" he asked.

She glared at him. "No. But I have hauled in a few six-pounders. And what if I land several of them?"

"We'll hitch them to the back of the truck and let them walk home," he mused.

They stopped beside the river. "I'll go back for the camp stools," he said. "Watch for snakes. They may be crawling early. Did you bring hip boots?"

She frowned. "I don't have any."

He sighed. "I'd offer a pair of mine, but you wouldn't be able to see over the cuffs," he added. "Shrimp."

"I am not a shrimp," she huffed. "I'm tall for my age."

"You're a shrimp." To emphasize it, he moved close, so that she had to look up to see his face.

He chuckled. "You really are small, compared to me," he said, and his voice dropped an octave, into deep dark velvet that made chills go down her spine. One big, beautiful hand came up to trace her jaw and her pretty bow mouth. His eyes dropped to it, studying it so intently that her lips parted on a quick breath.

"You stop that," she whispered, her voice unsteady. "Unless you want me to push you right down into the grass and do unspeakable things to you."

He laughed. "What sort of unspeakable things do you have in mind?"

She paused, because she didn't really know. Except for an occasional classic romance movie or a romance novel, she really had little idea about that part of men and women.

"Well?" he asked.

"I'm thinking, I'm thinking," she protested. "So many choices, so little time. Besides," she added, "there are people everywhere."

He pursed his lips. "So there are." He chuckled and dropped his hand. He went back to the truck while she tried to calm her heartbeat. She was a pushover, and he surely knew it. She hoped he had enough finer instincts to protect her from herself. If she had any defenses at all, they were weak and untrustworthy.

He was back with two camp stools. He opened one for her and set it up.

"Worms or flies?" he asked.

She stared at him.

"Well?"

She took a breath. "Grandad and I fished for bass mostly. I'm not really good at fishing for trout," she confessed uncomfortably. "And every time I ever tried to cast, like those guys are doing"—she indicated the poetry of movement coming from the fishermen wading in the shallow river, casting perfect lines far out into the fast-moving water—"I ended up having to be cut out of the fishing line at least once a trip."

He chuckled deep under his breath, his eyes amused and tender as he studied her.

"Then why did you want to come?" he asked.

She bit her lower lip. "Well," she began, hoping for inspiration.

While she was searching for it, he bent and brushed his mouth tenderly against hers, a whispery brief caress that made her knees go weak.

"Sit and watch. Pay attention. Quiz coming later," he added, and set about to put on waders and get his tackle affixed to the rod and reel.

It was educational. Obviously, this was something he'd been doing for a long time. It was fascinating to watch the line shoot out in lovely patterns before just the tip, with the fly and sinkers, met the water to tempt any fishy occupants of the river.

For the first hour, there were nibbles, but no catches. She sat and watched him, delighting in the grace of his tall, powerful body, in the economy of motion that accompanied each cast. He was slow and patient, never rushed or frustrated. He was intent on what he was doing, absolutely single-minded to a degree she'd never encountered in anyone else.

He was absolutely gorgeous. Jet-black hair, thick and with a sheen like a raven's wing, dark eyes under a jutting brow. High cheekbones, olive skin, and a mouth as chiseled and beautiful as any male movie star's. She couldn't get enough of just looking at him.

She knew it was going to be a disaster. He'd been badly hurt by the woman he loved, a woman with whom, by all reports, he was still in love. He wanted no involvement. In fact, he'd even said that loose ties were the only kind he ever wanted. Presumably, he wouldn't have married his former lover even if she'd been willing.

While Sara was a homebody, who loved working in the house, working on the ranch, having her little brother to care for. She had no inclination to travel, to be anything other than what she was—an artist with a happy home life, now that her abusive father was no longer around to terrify her and Ed.

It was a recipe for heartache. If she'd had any sense, she'd have refused his offer of transportation to Denver the very first time she'd been invited to go. But she hadn't. And every contact she had with the mysterious Mr. Blakeney, the worse it got, the more she was attracted to him.

He had a shady past, from all accounts. He dressed well. His truck was almost new. But he had no visible means of support. Yes, there was the ranch, but it was much like hers. Run-down, with just a few head of cattle and part-time help. The way he lived and his lack of income were a red flag. That disparity could indicate that he made his living outside the law. Danny Hartman had hinted as much.

A man who seemed to live above his means, who kept to himself, who had a past that he never talked about. There were a lot of red flags. Too many.

"Are you going to pour that, or sit and look at it?"

His voice startled her and she jumped. She hadn't heard him move. Amazing, how quiet he was in an area with things on the ground that made noise. But he didn't make noise.

"Sorry." She laughed nervously. "I wasn't paying attention. Want coffee?"

"Would I be standing here if I didn't?" he asked with raised eyebrows.

She made a face at him and poured coffee into one of the plastic mugs she'd packed. She handed it to him.

He noticed the faint tremor in her fingers. She had pretty hands. Long fingers, immaculate nails, well-kept despite the physical labor she did around her ranch. She was nervous when he went close to her. It pleased him in one sense and disturbed him in another. He couldn't afford to let her become attached to him. There were things he couldn't tell her about his life.

"You could stand up a spoon in this," he pointed out.

She was sipping the cup she'd poured for herself. "Oh, yes," she said. "I hate half-hearted hot brown water."

He grinned. "Me, too."

There was a loud, rough word from the other side of the river. It was followed by a lot more loud, rough words. They were followed by the speaker slamming his rod and reel onto the ground and then jumping on it, still cursing at the top of his lungs.

They burst out laughing along with two other men on their side of the river.

"It's not funny!" the owner of the trashed pole yelled

at his audience. He picked up his tackle box and stomped off toward his truck.

"Some people should never take up fishing. Old Duke Ramsey over there is a prime example of that," he pointed out.

"Why did he take it up, do you know?"

"Yes," he said. "His doctor said he was too stressed. He told Ramsey that fishing would relax him."

Which caused more laughter.

The two nearby fishermen left just before lunchtime. Neither had caught any fish. The men stopped just briefly to greet them, commiserate with them about the lack of biting trout, and went away.

"Finally," Blakeney mused, tying a different fly onto his line. "Now that I have the place to myself . . ."

He went off to the river, made a couple of casts, and came up with a magnificent fighting trout. Sara, delighted, went to the river to watch him fight the trout. He laughed and pulled and released, pulled and released, as he and the fish both began to tire. But finally, he caught it in the net he'd asked her to hand him. He slid it into the bucket with the lid and caught his breath.

"That was an epic battle! Are you worn out?" Sara asked.

"Just about . . . !"

She pushed him back into the grass and fell on him, laughing. "Trapped," she teased, bending to kiss him softly. "Now I've got you where I want you!"

His dark eyes twinkled as he looked up at her. "Oh,

have you?" he asked. Before she could formulate an answer, he'd flipped her onto her back and now it was he who had her pinned.

"Now," he said softly, searching her eyes, "who's trapped?"

CHAPTER 6

"I need to get to my phone," she managed breathlessly, while her heart threatened to choke her.

One dark eyebrow went up. "You need to what?" he asked.

"Get to my phone," she repeated.

"Why?"

"I haven't gotten to that chapter yet."

He blinked.

"I don't know what to do next," she said huskily. "It's in chapter five of my new book I bought. I haven't read it . . ."

He cocked his head. "And what kind of book would this be?"

"It just came out," she said. "It's an adventure novel."

"An adventure novel." He nodded.

"Yes, and the hero is very worldly and he gets mixed up with this elegant woman who turns out to be working for a gangster . . . !"

He was staring at her. "What does this have to do with that?" he asked, trying to maintain his composure.

Because he knew that story very well. Very well. Too well.

"The next chapter is where she pushes him down and does things to him," she explained. "I only skimmed a little ahead. I haven't actually read it yet, so I don't know what comes next."

He burst out laughing. He rolled over beside her, onto his back, and absolutely roared.

She hit him. "We aren't born knowing these things," she pointed out. "I was too busy at home to go running around with men, learning how to do intimate stuff. And television is useless. It's all messed up with people doing unspeakable things to other people . . . Honestly, I was better off mucking out the stable!"

He could barely get his breath. She had no idea that he knew exactly what came next in that book, and for a good reason.

"Will you stop laughing?" she chided, sitting up. "I'll bet you weren't born knowing all that stuff, either!"

"I wasn't," he managed, and finally sat up, shaking his head as he studied her. "You are a breath of spring."

"I'm a what?"

"Sara, I don't think there's another woman alive, even in Raven Springs, who doesn't know what comes next."

"They probably didn't have an alcoholic father, and a little baby to take care of, either," she reasoned.

"Probably not," he agreed, his eyes kind. "The sort of women in my life wouldn't have wasted an hour on a sick woman or a child."

She looked at him for a long time. "Why would you pick women like that?" she asked gently.

"Avoiding responsibility," he mused, his eyes on a hawk flying above. "I never wanted mundane things like marriage and kids. I wanted adventure. Excitement. I wanted exotic places and dangerous people."

Her heart sank. She'd known that already at some level. But hearing it was like having a door slammed in her face. He was a worldly man and she was a backwoods girl, with no real knowledge of the outside world other than what she'd learned on her two trips to Denver.

"I've never been out of our county in my life," she mused. "Except when I went to Denver with you."

He gaped at her. "What?"

"I had too much responsibility at home to do anything else," she reminded him. "And I never had any money."

"Didn't you want to travel, to see new places, meet new people?" he wondered.

"Of course, but I had no money and I couldn't leave Mama, and then Ed," she said simply. "So I got my adventure from reading Cyrus Truman's novels."

His heart jumped. He had to be careful. So he looked bewildered and asked, "Who?"

"Cyrus Truman," she repeated. "He's really famous. He writes those big adventure novels about espionage and foreign agents and gangsters all mixed up with politics and black ops," she explained. "Nobody knows where he gets his information. He knows about new things that haven't even been talked about in public." She laughed. "You should read one of his books. Honestly, they're all that kept me sane in the past few months when Daddy went on his last rampages. He was my hero." She lowered her eyes. "I guess that sounds stupid and naïve to you."

It sounded anything but. He hadn't thought of her as the sort of person who'd be interested in such things. He was surprised. She was a kindred spirit that he hadn't discovered until now.

"It doesn't sound stupid. Sometimes books are all we have to keep us sane," he agreed, and there was a faraway look on his face.

She cocked her head. "Our sheriff was overseas in the Middle East. They said you were, too, but not in the army, like Jeff."

His head turned slowly. He looked into her eyes. His were darker, almost black, as the memories hit him. Hard.

She reached out a small hand and put it on his forearm. "The past is just a memory. We can't go back and change anything. It's dangerous to try and live there," she added softly. "You have to move on and leave the nightmares behind."

His eyes took on a glitter. "You don't know a damned thing about my past," he said in a dangerously soft voice.

"I know that it haunts you," she said simply, and her heart was in her eyes. "And that it shouldn't. Things happen for reasons . . ."

He rolled his eyes. "And here we go with the sermon," he growled.

"No sermons," she said with a quiet smile. "The difference between you and me is that I put one foot in front of the other and go forward, every day, even if it's just one step. I'm no good for Ed if I live in the misery of my past. I have to think of him and how I can give him a better life than I've had."

His face was like stone. He stared at the horizon. "You have no idea what my past was like, what I've done . . ." He stopped abruptly.

Her fingers were caressing on his sleeve. "I don't need to," she said. "It's a part of you that you keep hidden deep inside, like a chest with no key. Maybe that's the best way to deal with it, for some people. No solution fits every situation."

He made a rough sound and pulled at a blade of grass. "I had a counselor who was furious that I wouldn't open up, as he called it, and tell him everything."

"There are good counselors and bad ones. And sometimes there are mismatched ones, who've never been in combat and have no understanding of what men survive in the field."

He frowned, staring at her. "How do you know that?"

"I couldn't travel, so I read. Book after book on spec ops, on Green Berets, on the SAS in England, on Army Rangers and the French Foreign Legion. Personal stories from men who'd been in combat." Her eyes were far away. "I learned so much. I learned about personal courage, and that being afraid is part of heroism. Everybody's afraid in combat; they all said that. But they take that fear and use it and go right through battles because they have to, because other men's lives depend on them." She smiled. "I read Cyrus Truman's books also," she added. "He's like all those special forces guys rolled into one author. Plus he has to have been all over the world, the way he describes all those exotic locales, like Tangier and Paris and Rome and Africa." Her eyes were dreamy.

"I'll never see those places, or have to carry a gun and go up against armed men. But I feel like I walked right beside him into all those desperate situations. He was my greatest inspiration while Daddy was at his worst. Cyrus Truman saved me from giving up and . . ." She stopped abruptly and moved her hand away from his arm.

He glanced at her. "Giving up, and what?" he asked.

Her shoulders rose and fell. She grimaced. "Taking my own life," she said simply, looking up into his dark eyes. "Daddy had knocked me down and hit me with the buckle on his belt, over and over until I was bleeding and screaming. When he'd worn himself out, he left my room. I locked the door. I had some of Mama's pills that the doctor had given her before she died, pills for pain. I'd saved them. I went into the bathroom . . ." The horror of what she'd almost done made her sick. She took a steadying breath. "I thought I could do it. But then I thought about a scene in one of Truman's books—*Red Vengeance*, I think. He was cornered in this seedy little bar in Tangier. He'd just survived a gunfight that left two very nasty men dead in a nearby building. He was on the run, but there were too many people after the shooter, so he had to find a way to leave the area. Plus the local police, who were very efficient, tracked the shooter to the seedy bar. It was very exciting," she added. "They came in the door, half a dozen of them, dressed in camo, carrying AK-47s. He could have tried to run, but he didn't. He sat right there, cool as ice, as they looked around for some desperate, sweating man who'd give himself away. They didn't know who they were looking for, but he'd just shot two men and they were sure that their quarry would look like a hunted, desperate man.

"But all they saw was several men drinking and having a good time. The hero had pulled the waitress down on his lap and put his arm around her. She knew what was going on, and cooperated. He was very handsome," she added with a grin. "So the police wandered past his table, and he just smiled at them and nonchalantly raised a glass. They gave him hardly a glance and kept walking. He bluffed them into leaving, because he kept his head." She laughed. "He got out of the bar and took a cab to the airport, just that easily. And I thought if he could do it, if he could survive against impossible odds like that, I can do it. At least, there weren't dozens of armed men hunting me. Just one mean, alcoholic father."

He smiled slowly. He remembered the trip that had inspired that novel. The experience had been more nerve-racking than he'd remembered. As he listened to her, he relived it.

Funny, he'd never considered what his readers felt when they read his books. Sara was giving him a whole new perspective on what readers thought about his adventures. He felt vaguely proud that he could inspire her enough to actually save her life.

"I never thought about readers' reactions to novels," he murmured.

"I don't imagine the author did, either," she said, oblivious to who he really was. "But he saved my life."

He smiled slowly. "Good for him."

She smiled back. "Books have been my only escape," she confessed. "The more adventurous, the better. I wanted to read things that would take me far away from my own problems." She looked up at him. "Isn't that what they call living vicariously?"

He nodded.

"Have you ever done that?" she wondered aloud.

"I do it a lot," he said, but, of course, he was writing from his own experiences. She didn't know that.

She sighed. "So many brave men," she mused. "And nobody even knows who they are. They're like shadows that pass us in the night and fade away."

"Nice description." He chuckled. "You should write books."

"Not me. I'm not smart enough, or experienced enough, or traveled enough. I'll let other people do those things and I'll buy books that tell about them," she said with a grin.

He studied her quietly. "How many of Truman's books do you have?" he wondered.

"Oh, all of them," she said. "Of course, I used to have to wait for the paperbacks to come out before I could afford them. I'd check them out at the library in hardcover and then I'd buy the paperbacks several months later. But I get them on e-book these days." She grinned. "Except now I can afford the hardcovers. I'll have my own collection. Those books are keepers."

"I'm sure Mr. Truman would be gratified to know that he had such an ardent fan," he told her.

"He's so famous that he doesn't need any more adulation than he already gets," she mused. "They said when he goes on tour, he has to have a bodyguard along to toss the women out of his room. Some of them actually bribed people to get them into his room when he was speaking at writers' conferences."

"Do tell." He could have told her some stories about that!

"It must be nice, being famous," she said, picking up a twig. "I don't know, though. I don't like crowds and I value my privacy. I'm not sure I'd like being notorious and having to have people chased out of my hotel room." She brightened. "But artists aren't quite so public as authors. Bestselling authors are like movie stars and TV personalities. Their faces are well-known. Artists are different. I like being a hermit."

"Most authors would like it, too. But publishers want their authors to go on tour. It sells more books. They also do media tours."

"Media tours?"

"Yes. They go to big studios, like in New York City, and the interviews are done with just a producer, a cameraman and a sound guy, and whatever host they're invited by. They're connected to TV shows all over the country."

"Wow. That sounds very exciting."

"Excitement, over time, turns tedious."

She sighed. "I guess it would. But if you're really famous, it sort of goes with the turf, doesn't it?" She stared at her drawn-up knees. "I wouldn't want to be that famous. But then, I just paint." She grinned at him.

"Just paint." He rolled his eyes. "Your work is genius. They told you that and it's the truth."

She smiled from ear to ear. "Thanks. But I can't really take credit for it. It's a gift. Something that comes through me more than it comes from me," she tried to explain.

"Like writing," he agreed at once. "One author described it as being on autopilot. She said she just typed the books. She had no idea what was coming next until she saw it on her computer screen."

"That's how I feel, too."

His eyes narrowed on her face. "You're wiser than your years."

"Shucks," she scoffed. "'T'ain't nothin'." She grinned widely.

He burst out laughing. "You got that from old man Riley Barnes."

"He doesn't mind. Everybody mimics him. He's a sweetheart."

He raised an eyebrow. "Am I a sweetheart?" he teased.

She cocked her head. "You're a barracuda in a tuna suit."

He chuckled. "You'll need to read the next chapter," he said.

She blinked, having forgotten their earlier conversation. "So you know what to do."

"What to . . ." She stopped and flushed at the look in his dark eyes.

He moved closer and in a lightning move, had her flat on her back. "But I can give you a few pointers . . ."

She opened her mouth to answer him and his lips came down on hers. Soft at first, tender, brushing and lifting in sweet little touches that made her body sing. She caught her breath as the fever began to burn in her, a new fever that was frightening in its intensity.

She shivered as his mouth became suddenly insistent. He smoothed his strong, hard body over hers, one long leg insinuating itself between both of hers. While his mouth ravaged hers, his hands smoothed up and down her rib cage, his thumbs lightly brushing her small, taut breasts with every sweep.

She was shocked when she felt him move again, so that he was right against her in a greater intimacy than she'd ever experienced in her life. His mouth became more insistent. His body moved roughly on hers, and she felt something she'd only read about before.

Her small hands pushed unsteadily at his chest. But he was in over his head. She was warm and sweet and heaven to kiss. He'd been months without a woman, and he was losing his self-control! He barely felt the protest.

She managed to drag her mouth away, shivering with need, not wanting to stop, but afraid to let it continue. She wasn't a casual lover and she wasn't going to be a convenience for any man, especially this one, who'd already made his views about permanence crystal clear.

"You have . . . to stop," she said brokenly. "I can't!"

"You can." His mouth was more insistent now, like the hips moving sensuously against her own.

"No," she said in a loud voice, and she dragged herself away from him and sat up, shivering.

He took deep breaths. He'd never felt such a loss of control. He didn't understand it, and he was furious. She was playing him for a fool. Why hadn't he realized? He sat up too, glaring at her. "Why not?" he asked curtly. "Everybody does it."

"Not everybody," she said with what was left of her dignity. "I'm sorry. I was playing earlier. I didn't mean to sound . . ."

"But that's how women play the game," he said in a cold, sarcastic tone. "Come closer, come closer, stop, no, I can't do that. Go away, but if you offer me a new Ferrari or some diamonds, I'll probably change my mind."

She turned her head and looked at him with sheer horror. "They do that to you?" she asked, shocked.

"Every woman does," he said. He got to his feet. "And you're no different," he added coldly. "What do you want?"

She got slowly to her feet and looked up at him. "I have everything I want," she said with quiet dignity. "And what I don't have, I work for."

He was breathing heavily. He was furious and trying to control it. His fists were clenched at his sides as he glared at her. "Teasing me about fishing, taking such interest in my past, in my nightmares." He laughed coldly. "Who told you?"

She blinked and frowned. "Told me what?" she asked, her face totally without guile.

Even in his fury, he recognized her lack of understanding. "It's a small town. People gossip. How can you not know about me?"

"Nobody gossips about you," she replied. "They're afraid to. Jeff warned them."

"Did he tell you?" he persisted.

"I don't know the sheriff that well," she replied. She drew in a breath. What had seemed like a quiet, wonderful fishing trip had turned into a disaster. "Can you drive me home, please?" she asked softly.

"Hell, yes." He got his tackle together, along with his one fish. She was in the truck, belted in and waiting, until he got in beside her. He started the truck and pulled out into the highway. Even furious, his control was absolute. He didn't speed or even scratch off.

Sara realized then that he'd only been kind to her because he needed a woman. She didn't understand much of what went on between men and women, except for what she'd read, but she'd made the mistake of taking Ty's kindness seriously. She'd thought he really did like her and wanted to get to know her. She should have had better sense. She wasn't really pretty, or sophisticated like they said his ex-girlfriend had been. She was only a body to him. Just that. It made her want to cry.

He pulled up at her steps. With her dignity just barely intact, she smiled at him. "Thanks for the fishing trip. It was nice."

"Liar." He said it coldly, and with a glittery glare. She kept the smile. "Goodbye."

He was on his way back to his own place before he realized what she'd said to her. Not "so long" or "see you later." She'd said, very firmly, "goodbye."

It should have made him happy. He was getting in too deep with her. He, who wanted no serious ties ever again.

Well, he'd ensured that there would never be anything serious with Sara. She'd assumed that all he'd wanted was a few nights in bed with her. Because that was what she'd inferred from his behavior.

Actually, it wasn't clear in his mind what he wanted, beyond kissing Sara until he couldn't stand up. Her mouth was soft and sweet. She was kind and caring. He was a man with a past, a dark past that haunted him, and Sara was an innocent.

He should be grateful that he'd found her out in time, before he was hooked. She knew too much about him. He didn't believe it was perception. Probably Jeff had told her about his past and she'd let him think she had mental powers or something.

She thought he only wanted her body. He wasn't sure what he wanted. He missed her when he was at home alone. He thought about her, far too much. He couldn't get the memory of her soft body in his arms out of his mind.

She wasn't like any of the women who'd passed through his life. The last one, his ex-fiancée, had been a hard-nosed opportunist. He knew she'd slept with Danny Hartman, who'd been delighted to share the experience with Ty, whom he despised. It had been the last straw for Ty, who'd raged at the woman for her disloyalty. That was when she'd laughed and told him about the rich accountant who'd proposed to her. He was far richer than Ty. His parents were very rich and he was an only child. Besides that, he didn't live on a ramshackle ranch in the middle of nowhere.

She wanted glitter and high society and lots and lots of money to spend. Ty had been so besotted with her at first that he hadn't minded her flaws. But as time went by, she was more dissatisfied, more belligerent, more demanding. He did have money, but it was tied up in stocks and bonds and land and charitable foundations. He had little ready cash. She didn't know just how rich he was. She'd heard that he wrote novels, and she'd asked him about it. But he'd told her it was only category stuff, just for men. He'd wanted her to want him for who he was, not what he had. She was great in bed. Not much out of it. She took him at face value, unaware of who he really was, and she'd let the accountant sweet-talk her into running away with him.

Meanwhile, since she'd left him and married the accountant, somebody had told her who Ty Blakeney really was—a powerhouse of a bestselling, world-class author. Now she'd lost her husband to a smarter woman and she was between men. She was trying to come back. Weeks ago, he might have been stupid enough to let her.

But now, after Sara's gentle influence, he was a

different man. The past had retreated without him realizing it. He was looking ahead, not back. He liked just being with Sara. She was more than a possible conquest. She was fun to be with. She had a huge heart. She took care of her little brother with great care, when a less principled woman might have just given him up to the protective services and led her own life. But that wasn't Sara. She was loyal. Self-sacrificing. Loving.

He felt those thoughts like a body blow. She'd had feelings for him. He knew it, but hadn't shamed her by throwing it at her. She wanted him, too, although she didn't seem to understand that, either. She was a green girl, totally naïve and clueless about modern life. She was the sort of woman his late mother would have taken in and loved without a single doubt. She would have loved Sara.

When he got home, he just sat in the truck for a few minutes, thinking about what he'd done. It began to sink in that Sara would never let him near her now. She'd be polite if they met, but she'd never allow him close enough to hurt her again. He'd ridiculed her, cheapened her, shredded her pride. She wouldn't forget that.

He remembered what she'd told him about wanting to die after her father had beaten her, that his book had brought her back from the brink of disaster. She'd idolized him. And what had he done? Made fun of her attraction to him, shamed her with his idea of why she'd teased him. He'd humbled her, in the worst way, because she'd been attracted to him. And for what?

Fear. That was why he'd pushed her away. He'd

been thrown out like garbage by a woman he loved. He was determined that he'd never let that happen again. Not registering that Sara was as unlike his former fiancée as the moon was from Mars, he'd found a way to push her out of his life before he went in headfirst and couldn't save himself. He wasn't going to be sucked into her life.

He'd won. She got out of the truck as she got out of his life. It wasn't that she didn't forgive. It was that she pulled into her shell like a turtle and stayed there to avoid being hurt. She was the kindest woman he'd ever known. And he'd treated her like a streetwalker who didn't want to take his money.

He leaned his head against the steering wheel. It felt cool and comforting while he contemplated what was left of his life. The road ahead would be empty and without color. The one person who made it beautiful was now gone, and it was his own fault.

He'd always said he was better, and safer, alone. Now he had a chance to prove it. He'd removed the one obstacle that could have taken him beyond his agony, into the light. He should be throwing confetti and sending up fireworks. Hooray, no more Sara to threaten his solitude.

He got out of the truck and walked slowly up the path to his cabin. The sky looked angry and cold. So did his future. He felt a chill that had nothing to do with weather, like icy footprints on his heart.

* * *

Sara spent a miserable day smiling and pretending that everything was all right. She thanked Mrs. Grimes for babysitting the puppy, gave her a check, and left her and Ed, when Sara brought him home, playing video games while she worked in the kitchen making them lunch.

"It's tuna fish sandwiches with homemade french fries," she announced. "And vanilla pudding for dessert."

"Sounds lovely," Mrs. Grimes said.

"I have to finish this battle before I can quit," Ed said, glancing worriedly at his sister.

She just smiled. "Go ahead, it will keep." She went back into the kitchen, where she'd confined Goose to keep him from helping himself to the sandwiches on the coffee table.

Later, after she'd put Ed to bed, she climbed in under the covers in her own bed, the one she'd had since she was ten years old. It was comforting somehow. She'd always run in here to hide when her father went on his rampages. Most of the time, she could get the door locked before he could hit her. Most of the time.

She thought about what Ty had told her, about the little baby who'd died and sent her father almost crazy with guilt and grief. She could understand a little more why he drank. But the way he took out his guilt on his two remaining children had been terrible. Her poor sick mother had lived in terror, like her son and daughter. The sheriff would lock up her father infrequently, and that gave her mother and Ed and Sara just a little respite until he came home again. Those few peaceful days and nights were like diamonds in mud.

She put the dirty dishes in the dishwasher and cleaned the kitchen. It gave her something to do to take her mind off her disastrous date with Ty. She could never face him again. It would be too humiliating. His opinion of her stung like a wasp.

Mrs. Grimes came into the kitchen directly with plates and glasses that had held milk.

"Can I help?" she asked gently.

Sara smiled. "No, but thank you. I'm almost through in here."

"That wasn't what I meant," the older woman said, putting her burden in the sink. She straightened back up and looked at Sara with quiet sympathy. "I said I had a nice shoulder, you know," she added softly.

Sara went into her arms and cried like a child.

"I told you about Ty," she said, her voice comforting. "It's always the worst men we set our hearts on. My first boyfriend was in a motorcycle gang, one of the really mean ones. I found all sorts of excuses for him until he ran over a little girl and laughed when her legs were broken. It opened my eyes."

Sara drew back and wiped her eyes on the hem of her T-shirt. "I should have known better," she said. "I thought he liked being with me. I never dreamed that it was all a means to an end . . ." She broke off, embarrassed.

"Same thing happened to me with a man," Mrs. Grimes said, not even shocked. "I thought he liked me, too." She sighed. "And that was almost forty years ago, but I still remember how crazy I was about him. I would have done anything for him. But what he did opened my eyes, just in time. Why do we always love the bad boys?"

"If you can find out, please tell me. I'm so naïve, I belong in the twentieth century!"

"I know the feeling, believe me. When you're my age, you look around and realize it's not your world anymore. You'll understand better one day, when you're older."

"I already understand it." She sighed.

"Ty has lived through some bad times. Worse than I can even tell you." She indicated the bookshelves, which were full of first-person accounts of great battles, of special forces, of international politics and their repercussions. "Well, if you've read those books, you already know what he's been through."

Sara gaped at her, her mouth falling open in surprise.

Mrs. Grimes nodded. "He was in one of those black ops programs. Don't ask. That's all I really know for sure. He has a cousin who's in the Russian mafia, and contacts in some really bad places. I don't think he works outside the law, but even if he does, he has pull in the Capitol. People who cross him, or his bosses, end badly."

"But he's not like that," Sara protested. "He's a good man."

Mrs. Grimes smiled. "Yes, he is. He has a conscience, despite the fact that they did their best to beat him out of it. He interrupted a mission that would have resulted in the deaths of several children, and threatened to go in front of a Senate investigating committee and tell the whole story. Naturally, they did nothing. He can be fearful when he wants to, and that time he had proof."

"I noticed that he hates injustice," Sara said, averting her eyes.

"He's not too keen on women right now, either," Mrs. Grimes added. "So keep that in mind if you have any more dealings with him."

"That's unlikely," Sara said, without elaborating. "I don't think he'll ever come near me again."

"And you'll never even whisper the reason why."

Sara just nodded.

Mrs. Grimes picked up a shirt she'd been mending for Ed. "Well, sometimes things seem to be at a dead end. And then the hero finds a piece of twine and a paper clip and lets himself out of his cell just before he's due to be executed."

"Really?" Sara exclaimed.

"Really. I'll tell you the story one day. Right now," she said, putting down the mended shirt, "I'm going home to get some housework done. Something you might like to do also," she added gently. "Staying busy helps."

Sara smiled wearily. "You know, that's the best idea I've heard today!"

Mrs. Grimes smiled. "Everything will be all right," she said. "You have to believe that."

Sara sighed. "I'll do my best."

"That's all anyone can promise," the other woman said, turning back to the living room to get her things together.

* * *

Days went by. Sara buried herself in her art, painting new canvases that were stormy and chaotic, ones that mirrored the pain and distance inside her that could find no safe harbor. She did her best not to think about the cause of them.

Meanwhile, she took Ed on field trips around the county, and to parties with other children at the church they attended. It kept her mind off things. Sort of.

The object of her misery was doing the same thing. He was working, for the first time in months. This novel was about a bad man who got himself involved with a small-town girl who was innocent and caring. He hadn't planned to write any such thing, but the words kept coming. It was one of those books that literally wrote itself. All he had to do was sit at the computer and put his fingers on the keys. The book unfolded page by page.

He saw Sara at a distance in town from time to time. At the bank. At the pharmacy. Once he saw her coming out of the coffee shop. She saw him as well. She only smiled and nodded and went about her business. He had no idea how difficult it was for her to do that, and look normal, when inside she was wilting like a flower that had not been watered.

He was pretending as well. Pretending that Sara was still part of his life, that he could take her fishing or just riding around. That he could sit and talk to her.

Once, she had to go to Denver on business. But rather than ask Ty, she bought a small compact car and drove herself. It was a harrowing experience, driving in traffic, but she managed to do it without wrecking the car.

Once, when she ran into the sheriff at the local diner, he walked out with her and asked if she knew about her father's connection with Ty Blakeney. She hadn't. It turned out that they were in the same combat area overseas. Although Ty was much younger, Sara's father had been the officer in charge of an army company stationed where Ty was involved in black ops. Ty had saved her father's life.

It was a shock. She hadn't known there was any connection. The sheriff, who'd also been in the army unit with her father, explained that a lot of her father's problems could be blamed on the things he'd seen and done in combat. It changed men, he told her. Changed them in terrible ways sometimes. She was grateful for the information. It helped explain a lot.

Life rocked on. Spring came and went, with new clothes and toys for Ed and new clothes and some new calves for Sara. They gave Mrs. Grimes a gift card for her birthday. Sara was still mourning Ty and trying to shut him out of her mind. He hadn't come near her for months. She never expected him to again, either. As time passed, things got a little easier. But only a little.

CHAPTER 7

Ty had a job overseas that took three months out of his busy schedule. He'd finished the hardcover novel that was to be released in the spring of the following year, books generally being produced a year in advance of publication. It had been a hectic thing, with the side trip, but he and his editor had met the deadline.

He'd dedicated it to Sara.

He thought about nothing else as time went by. He saw her occasionally, but she was like a wisp in the wind that he was unable to capture. Once he'd tried to talk to her, but she'd just smiled and excused herself and kept walking. Once burned, twice shy. He understood why she avoided him. It still hurt. So did his conscience.

Sara was feeling her own discomfort. Ty had become a big part of her life. She didn't understand why he'd gone from a friend to an enemy in such a short time. Mrs. Grimes said he was fighting his own feelings for her. Sara didn't believe it. If he'd cared, he wouldn't have stayed away so long.

What she didn't know was that he was making plans

that included her. He was giving up his dangerous lifestyle. It was difficult, because he was obligated for two missions that he couldn't back out of. But he'd made himself a solemn promise that he was going to live a normal life from now on. Go on tour with the books. Maybe raise a few cattle. Write a lot of books. And just live life. He had more than enough material to write about for the rest of his life.

Now, he just wanted to get back to Sara.

Danny Hartman had phoned her once or twice, offering trips to the theater or opera in Denver, but she'd turned down every invitation. She had no interest in a relationship with a man she ardently disliked. Besides that, he didn't like Ed, and vice versa. Nobody was going to come into her life who didn't want her little brother around.

"Sis, why don't we ever see Mr. Blakeney anymore?" Ed asked out of the blue one afternoon while he was playing games on the console and Sara was sketching an idea for a new canvas.

Her hand slipped on the sketching pad. She erased madly. "What do you mean? We saw him in town just the other day," she reminded him, while inside she was quivering like a jelly.

"You know what I mean. He really liked you."

"I'll tell you when you're twenty-five," she promised.

He laughed. "Okay. But remember, you promised."

"Cross my heart," she replied, and did that.

* * *

Her dreams were wild and savage. Most of them contained Ty. She wished that she could just forget him. Once or twice, she'd entertained the idea of moving away, to some other small town where she wouldn't have to see him.

She'd mentioned it to Doris, the owner of the local bookstore, who was also a casual friend.

"You can't move away from problems." The other woman sighed. "They just go with you. Oh, you read Truman, don't you?" she added, pulling out a hardcover from the new releases shelf. "You should look at this!"

She handed the book, open, to Sara. The dedication said, *"To Sara, who inspired it."*

Her heart jumped into her throat, at the words, but logic stuffed it back down. She handed the book back. "It's a coincidence. A big-time author like that wouldn't even notice somebody like me," she said, smiling. "I don't even know Cyrus Truman. It's somebody he knows well."

Doris frowned. "Surely you know."

"Know what?"

"I can't believe you've lived here all your life and you don't know about Ty Blakeney. Honestly, he was always taking you places last year!"

Sara frowned. "What don't I know about him?"

"He writes books under a pen name. The pen name is Cyrus Truman," Doris told her.

Sara felt as if every cell in her body had exploded. She leaned against the counter, trying to get her breath.

"And there's only one Sara around here that Ty Blakeney has been seen with," Doris added with a grin.

"I don't understand," Sara said nervously. She glanced at Doris. "Honestly, I haven't even seen him for months . . ."

"Nobody has. He's overseas. Some hush-hush mission," Doris replied. "He's due home soon, though."

Sara was still trying to absorb the shock. "Wow," she said finally. She had to read that book.

"Do you have a copy of it that you can sell me or is that only a promotional copy?" Sara asked huskily.

"I have many of them to sell. He's got a huge reading audience locally. Here." She handed the book to Sara, who promptly paid for it, thanked her friend, and walked out of the bookstore almost in a daze.

When she picked up Ed from his class, he was concerned.

"Are you okay, sis?" he asked worriedly. "You don't look like yourself."

"I'm not myself. At least, not right now. I'll tell you when we get home."

They were in the living room when she pulled the hardback out of the bag and handed it to Ed. "Read the dedication."

"I can't read a lot of big words yet," he told her.

"Try."

He sighed. "Okay." He looked at the words and sounded them out. He looked up. "It's you."

She nodded.

"Do you know this guy? I know you have all his books . . ."

"He's really Ty Blakeney," she said. "This is his pen name."

Ed was stunned. "He writes books?"

She nodded again. "He writes books. I'm going to read this one tonight, so you're going to bed early."

"Aw, sis," he complained.

"You can take your Game Boy to bed with you," she compromised.

He grinned. "Fair enough!"

She did read the book. It was, as usual, a roller coaster ride of a novel, full of espionage, spy versus spy, deadly attacks, and high-level politics. In between, it was a love story. The hero fell in love with a small-town girl who was everything he didn't want in a woman. But she turned out to be the only real thing in his life.

When she finished it, she was in tears. It was their story. It was what might have been. Was that why he'd dedicated it to her?

She put it on her bedside table and turned out the light. Perhaps it was just as well that he'd written the whole thing out of his system. She'd been trying to do that, all the lonely months since their ill-fated fishing trip, but with little success.

"Maybe I should write a book." She sighed as she closed her eyes.

* * *

"Did you hear?" Mrs. Grimes asked one Friday after she'd been babysitting Ed and Goose while Sara went to see a potential client.

"Hear what?" Sara asked as she put her purse on the table. She looked elegant in a pale silver silk dress with patches of subtle pastel colors. It was late summer, and the dress was cool and comfortable.

"Ty Blakeney's back."

Sara jumped. It wasn't obvious, more like a tiny reflex, but her whole body felt electrified.

"Is he? In one piece?"

"So they say. He's going on tour for this new book."

"*Devil's Pawn*," she said, naming it.

Mrs. Grimes grinned. "He dedicated it to you."

"That's not me," Sara said stubbornly. "It must be some other woman, maybe the one who threw him over." She looked down. "He's barely spoken to me."

"Miracles happen every day," Mrs. Grimes said smugly, looking past Sara to the open window. "Sometimes when you least expect them. My, my, look there, you've got company."

Sara turned. A pickup truck was stopping at the front door. A tall man wearing jeans and a black T-shirt got out of it.

"Ed, let's go play with the Game Boy in the kitchen with Goose," Mrs. Grimes said, tugging Ed to his feet and disappearing.

Sara went to the door like a sleepwalker.

She opened it before Ty could knock. They stood, just looking at each other.

"I tried to call you," he said after a minute. "But I figured you'd hang up the minute you heard my voice."

She nodded sadly, her eyes meeting his.

"Then I thought I might write to you, but I had visions of burning mail," he continued, smiling.

She shrugged and smiled, too.

"Finally, I thought if you read Cyrus Truman, you'd understand that the dedication in *Devil's Pawn* was meant for you."

She swallowed. "I didn't." She drew in a breath. "You probably know ten woman named Sara."

He searched her eyes hungrily. "No. I don't." He drew in a breath. "Sometimes we chase away the things we want most, because we're afraid we can't keep them," he said huskily.

She drew in a long breath, tears stinging her eyes. "Yes." Her voice broke on the word. "I thought . . . I'd never see you again . . ."

He drew her up tight and kissed her until her mouth was sore, and then he kissed her some more.

"When did you know that Truman was my pen name?" he asked finally, when he was sitting on the sofa with her in his lap, cradled in his arms.

"At the bookstore, when the book came out. Doris thought you dedicated it to me. I didn't know who you were until she told me."

He brushed back her wavy dark hair. "I wanted you to see a rancher instead of a famous author when we went around together," he said simply.

She smiled. "I'm no gold digger. Besides, I'm rich, too."

He laughed softly. "In which case, we should make plans to be together for a long, long time," he whispered against her mouth.

"What sort of plans?" she whispered.

"White dresses, lace, veils, black tie, ministers . . . that sort of plans."

She drew back a little, her eyes on his.

"I'm greedy," he said quietly. "I want forever."

She nodded. "Me, too."

He pulled a small box out of his pocket. "I bought them in Tangier. If you don't like them . . ."

She opened the box. They were rubies—her favorite stones—in a beautiful setting with a ruby solitaire that was at least three carats. She gasped. "But they're . . . they're magnificent!"

He chuckled. "You might go ahead and put on the solitaire. Just to see if it fits."

She did, and it did. She looked up at him. "You have to wear one, too," she said firmly. "I remember all about those women having to be evicted from your hotel rooms when you're on tour!"

"I will," he promised. "But you'll be right beside me when I go on tour, so I think other women will get the idea rather quickly."

She just looked at him, her heart in her eyes. "Oh, I love you," she whispered.

He bent and brushed his lips tenderly over her forehead. "And I love you. I didn't want to"—he sighed—"but sometimes victory lies hidden in defeat."

She grinned. "That's a nice line. You should put it in a book."

He chuckled. "I might do that."

Mrs. Grimes stuck her head around the door. "Is it safe to come back in?"

"Yes. We're going to get married," Ty told her.

"You can be my matron of honor," Sara told Mrs. Grimes.

"Can I be a flower boy?" Ed asked, and ran to hug Ty tightly.

"You can carry the ring," Ty told him. "It's a position of great honor."

"I'll do a good job," Ed promised. Ty hugged him close.

Sara just smiled, with her whole heart in her eyes.

And so they were married. The chapel was covered up in all sorts of beautiful roses. They spoke their vows with almost the whole town of Raven Springs, and half of Benton, in attendance. And the sheriff, Jeff Ralston, was Ty's best man.

Later, in a hotel room in Tangier, Sara practiced that chapter in Cyrus Truman's book that she'd been studying ever since *Devil's Pawn* was released.

She was drenched in sweat despite the air conditioning, disheveled, nude, and absolutely satisfied from head to toe as she looked at her husband's beaming face above hers.

"Did I get it right?" she asked breathlessly.

He chuckled. "You got it exactly right, my darling,"

he whispered, and kissed her again. He groaned and rolled over onto his back. "Talk about unbearable pleasure . . ." he said.

"You said I shouldn't be afraid, but I was. Sort of. At first." She whistled. "Only at first." She glared at him. "All those women in those books . . . !"

He put a finger over her mouth and grinned at her. "Lies. All lies. Honest. I have a great imagination."

"Lies," she countered with mock anger.

He made a face. "Okay, then, research. Only research! I write books, you know."

She laughed uproariously. It wasn't all lies—of course it wasn't—but she was far too happy to be jealous of women who were truly in the past. And they had, after all, contributed to Sara's own delightful first time. She could overlook a few things, in the interest of peace.

She melted into his side, sliding one silky leg over his powerful one. "All those beautiful women"—she sighed—"and you settled for a plain Jane like me."

"There is nothing plain about my wife," he said firmly. "She's unique. One of a kind. And I'm the luckiest man in the world."

She smiled, and kissed his shoulder. "I'm lucky, too. I never dreamed we'd end up like this." She sighed.

"Neither did I. Now I can't understand why I fought it so hard."

"You didn't want to be hurt. Neither did I. We were both looking for escape routes."

He nodded, his arm contracting around her shoulders. "But in the end, we got it right."

She smiled. "Just right." She cuddled closer. "Ty, about Ed," she began worriedly, because they hadn't discussed it in the breakneck run-up to the wedding.

"Ed will grow up in a loving household with happy people and a destructive but beautiful dog, and in a few years he'll have company to play video games with," he said gently.

Relief washed over her. She should have known. He'd even loved Goose at first sight, much less Ed. "He will?" She smiled mischievously. "You planning to start a gaming group?"

He chuckled and drew her up closer. "I had in mind a few smaller versions of ourselves. Little people who'll look like us."

She beamed at him. "I'd like that. I can teach them to paint."

"I'll teach them to write."

"We can both teach them to play video games," she added. "And to fish for trout . . ."

"All those things," he agreed, rolling her back over, his dark eyes twinkling. "But just at the moment, I have a few more things that I'd like to teach you . . ."

His mouth covered hers very slowly, and she didn't make any more comments. Not for a long, long time.

Outside the hotel room, the moon over Tangier shone discreetly through the window, right on the two happiest people in the world at that moment, in each other's arms. In each other's lives. In each other's hearts.

And they owed it all, every bit of it, to a furry little wuppie who'd brought them together.

A happy little wuppie, who was sleeping beside his boy, who was dreaming of Christmas, when he'd dress up his puppy as a reindeer, with a special Christmas collar . . . back home in Colorado.

CHRISTMAS, CRIME, AND A COWBOY

HEATHER GRAHAM

CHAPTER 1

Cows.

Jessy had nothing against cows.

She had simply never thought she'd be living surrounded by hundreds of creatures.

And horses, of course. But as she drove down the lonely—barely paved—road that led to the Danson ranch, she reminded herself she didn't have to *live* here; she could make all the right arrangements to keep the ranch going and then head straight back to New York City.

She smiled to herself, shrugging inwardly. There were those who might be horrified by the prospect of living in a place that was surrounded by giant buildings, the constant shriek of horns, and enough traffic to draw curse words from a nun.

But she'd grown up in New York. She loved New York. She'd gone to college in NYC; and while in her business a degree wasn't everything, she had loved her years at the university. And she had been employed by the McTavish Publishing Company before she'd even graduated, and while she didn't need to live in New York to keep working for them . . .

The city was filled with inspiration! Museums, art galleries, theaters . . . so much that stirred the artistic soul!

And here . . .

Seriously.

How the hell long could she draw cows?

Of course, it wasn't that she hadn't seen cows—or her family ranch—before. She had loved the ranch, too, mainly because she had adored her grandfather. He had been the first one to regale her with stories, to teach her to tell stories with pictures of puppies, kittens, and . . .

Yes, horses. And even cows.

More than that, she had simply loved her grandfather. He was the strongest human being she had met, a man whose very strength had allowed him to be extra kind, to respect every other human being, and to have care for any animal.

He raised horses. Prized quarter horses, exceptionally fit for all the different rodeos and shows that took place in this part of Colorado. And he had all the right people in place—Cody, his ranch manager. Plus, of course, the other Danson employees: Eddie, Tate, and David, the ranch hands who worked with Cody; Samantha, who managed the house; and Jenson Applegate, who handled all the business transactions. They had all been with Kelly for years before his death, and they were probably just waiting for her to give the go-ahead for them to continue as they were doing. Maybe they needed raises; that was fine. She believed in hard work being a great cause for a raise.

And, of course, the care of the animals was covered.

The good doctors James, Laura, Donald, and Yvonne covered the care of all the animals on the ranch, from horses to dogs to any bird that managed to get hurt on the property. Her grandfather made sure that "all creatures, great and small" received care when injured.

He really had been a great man, Jessy thought. Great in the strength that always allowed for kindness.

Hmm . . .

Except she wasn't sure why he had left her the note, written years before his death at the ripe old age of ninety-five. In the note he begged her to take and love the ranch and keep it running as it was something that had mattered so very much to him, and it was something that she would discover to be her heritage, something that she loved, too!

Loved even more than the towering buildings, hustle and shove, and downright deafening noise of the city.

She managed to smile. He'd known that she loved him as he had loved her, his only grandchild. He had also known that with such a note, he could manipulate her. But just so that he could be certain, a stipulation in his will had said she must come and sign papers and make future arrangements in person.

"Well, Grampa, I'm coming out!" she murmured aloud.

She passed the McFarlane property, and as she did so, she remembered an incident from the summer she had visited before her thirteenth birthday, something that had put a bit of a snag in her dining choices to this day.

Her grandfather had been making rodeo plans with

Brian McFarlane, and she'd been standing by one of the pastures. One cow had come up to her, and she had found herself stroking the animal's ears. Then a calf came up and another calf . . .

And then she'd gasped with horror, backing away.

They were creatures someone was going to eat!

But Wyatt McFarlane, about sixteen at the time, had come out of the house laughing at her.

"Don't worry! My dad only raises dairy cows. Trust me. The cows don't care if you drink milk or eat cheese!"

Laughing at her. Yeah, well, he'd been so cool as a teenager and was on the football team, Mr. Exceptionally Good-looking with his dark hair and startling blue-green eyes. He'd also made the grades to send him on to Yale; and besides being so physically handsome, naturally he'd played the guitar and excelled in music.

Now . . .

Well, she hadn't seen him in almost a decade now, not since she'd been a skinny and awkward teenager herself and he had been a college man, getting dual degrees in business and music.

Well, she'd gone on herself! She was an accomplished artist with a dozen illustrated novels for children on the market, as well as a few graphic novels for adults!

But the one reason she could never forget that day when she'd been petting cows had to do with the fact that she had become a pescatarian. Since she had gotten her diving license and had loved many a vacation in the Caribbean—as much as she loved New York, she didn't dive in the rivers or even in the waters of the Northeast coast—she'd seen the pretty vicious way that fish often ate fish.

She'd never seen a cow consume another!

Maybe it was all just stupid. But . . . whatever! She was here, she'd sign the papers, and she'd come back! After all, she'd visited her grandfather every year, at least until he'd gotten so sick the last months and come to New York to be with his family—her mom, dad, and her—through his last days.

And she knew, of course, why the ranch had been left to her and not her dad. Jessy loved her father with all her heart, but a stroke had left him in a wheelchair, and he was still struggling with his own health issues. She knew, too, that her father and grandfather had talked; her father had wanted the property to be left to her rather than him.

"Thanks, Dad," she said, speaking aloud again. Of course, she loved her father, too, and knew he wanted to come out to the ranch again. And he would do so when the doctors had cleared him to travel. She spoke out loud to herself again. "So! Almost—"

Almost . . . !

She almost *said "almost home!"*

"No, no, no!"

Once again, she spoke aloud, as if sound was necessary to verify the fact she wouldn't be here long.

But even as she spoke, a giant dog leaped out in front of her, having sailed over a fence from the McFarlane property.

She slammed on her brakes just in time to avoid the animal. But having cleared the fence and reached the road, the dog started running in circles in front of her car while wagging its tail and woofing.

"Bandit!"

Even in her air-conditioned car, she heard the roar of a male voice and saw that a man was racing after the dog, leaping the fence with ease as well.

She frowned, waiting for the man and the dog to move off the road. Then she realized she knew the man.

It was Wyatt McFarlane.

He turned and saw her in the rental car and gave her a surprised smile as he slipped a leash to the collar of the mammoth dog.

The dog wagged its tail wildly, apparently thrilled by the presence of the man who had caught up with him.

Man and dog approached her window. Wyatt leaned over against the car as she lowered her window. He obviously intended to speak to her.

"Jessy! Jessy Danson. Welcome home. Of course, I'm sorry, so sorry about your granddad. He was . . . well, of course, I loved him, too. He was like an amazing grandfather to me as well," Wyatt said.

She nodded and attempted a smile. "Yes, thank you. I know. He thought very highly of you. But he told me we weren't to mourn. He'd had a long and beautiful life, and he was ready for peace and believed in God. He'd be rejoined with the grandmother I was never able to meet."

"Well, it's great you're moving here, and you're going to be taking over the ranch," he said.

She tried to keep smiling. "I'm not staying. I mean,

I'll see to it that Grampa's people keep things running well, but I'm not moving out here."

"Ah, can't leave the city lights, eh?" he asked. "Well, too bad for us! You'd have been a welcome addition to the community."

"Thanks," she murmured. She found herself wondering about him. She knew he'd graduated from Yale about five years ago—she'd heard her parents and grandfather talking about the fact that he could have gone pro, but that he'd considered football a game that was great and that it was fun while he was in high school and college, but not at all what he wanted to do with his life. Then again, from what she understood, he wasn't using his music degree, either—other than playing in local cafés and sometimes showing up somewhere on a bigger stage.

No . . .

The man had come home after all that. To raise cows.

It wasn't going to happen to her!

By then the massive dog had come to the window, still madly wagging its tail and slobbering all over the window.

That was all right. She loved dogs. And it was a rental.

"Oh, come on now, Bandit!" he admonished the dog.

"That's all right," Jessy said quickly. "What is he? I don't think I've ever seen a bigger dog!"

"The vet says he's a mix between an English mastiff and a Great Dane and maybe something else," Wyatt told her with a shrug. "Someone ditched him in one of the big trash bins behind Murphy's Pub—you know the place in town. Brian Murphy heard him crying when he went in to open. He lives in town in an apartment, nowhere to keep such a massive animal, so . . ." He broke off, grimacing. "He didn't want to call animal control. He called me, and I went to pick him up and . . . here he is! I mean, yeah, he looks like a giant bear or something, but he's the sweetest guy in the universe. The only danger with him is he might love someone to death."

Jessy had to smile at that.

"Come out. Meet him properly. He can have manners," Wyatt told her.

She shrugged.

What difference did it make? Dusk was just starting to fall, and the lawyers weren't due at the Danson ranch until noon the next day.

She got out of the car. She was about five-eight herself, but the massive dog stood almost as tall as she did while he was on all fours.

"Wow, this guy is ready for the *Guinness Book of World Records*!" she said, stroking the animal's head. He moved forward as if to give her a big sloppy kiss.

"Manners, Bandit!" Wyatt said.

The dog sat and offered Jessy a massive paw. She laughed and shook his paw and found herself wondering about Wyatt again. His parents were alive and well, to the best of her knowledge. But here he was, and it looked like he was working at and for the ranch. Then again, everyone wore jeans and tailored cotton shirts or T-shirts around here and, with Christmas and true winter close on the horizon, denim jackets.

"Bought your latest book," he told her. "Gave one to my little cousin, Tabitha. It was adorable. Didn't really understand it all. You're listed as a paper engineer and artist."

She smiled. "I set it all up for the pop-ups—so the art is in position to be cut and turn into the right things, along with being the artist on that book."

"*Kitty the Kitten Finds a Home*," he said, reminding her of the title. "Really cute."

"Thanks." She realized she was still stroking Bandit's head, her own tilted a little so she could look up at Wyatt as they spoke. He hadn't changed much. Or maybe he had. He was a man now, still just as striking, his jaw a bit more solid, his rakish hair a little shorter, but his smile still intact.

And too charming.

Okay, time to move on!

"Well, great to see you, Wyatt—" she began.

"How long are you staying?" he asked, interrupting her.

"I guess at least a few days," she said. "But I do want to get home for Christmas."

"The tree at Rockefeller Center and all," he said lightly.

"No, you must have heard. My dad isn't in great health, either. I mean, we believe he's going to pull out and do fine, but he's not supposed to travel right now. I want to be home with him. I'm sure he wishes he could be here, but . . ." She left off with a shrug.

"Yes, I understand," he said. "I'm sorry to hear he hasn't been well. He's as nice a man as your grand-dad was."

"Thanks," she murmured. "I should get going."

"Right, sorry! Bandit and I didn't mean to waylay you."

"No, no, it was great to see you again, too, of course," she told him. "I . . . it's just hard, you know. Grampa loved this place so much, and he was so proud of leaving me this kind of an inheritance, and . . ."

"And you hate cows and love New York City," he said, grinning.

"First off, I don't hate cows—" she began.

"That's right! Are you still a pescatarian?" he asked her.

"Yeah. Sometimes I even feel guilty about the fish, except that when I'm diving, I see them eating each other all the time. But yeah, I'm still a pescatarian." She made a face. "I have a friend who loves to tell me that lobsters are in a very strange way related to cockroaches."

Wyatt laughed. She'd forgotten just *how* striking and likeable the man could be. No, maybe she hadn't. All the time she'd known him before, the few years' age difference between them had been major. But now, they were both adults, and three years was nothing; they'd both lived lives that had granted them maturity and . . .

No, no, no.

She wasn't going to allow herself to remember that she'd always had something of a crush on the man.

He wasn't really any part of her life. Just a piece of the past.

"Cockroaches, eh? Yummy!" Wyatt teased. "Well, there's not a lot of diving out here," he said dryly. "Then again," he murmured, frowning before asking her, "you do a lot of diving in NYC?"

She laughed. "No, I do a lot of dive vacations. I got into it years ago when I was still a senior in college, and I was hired for a kids' book about a friendly shark."

"And you found a friendly shark?" he asked dubiously.

"I made my creature a nurse shark. They're bottom guys and not aggressive. There's even a guy in the Florida Keys who has trained a pack of them—and rays—to play with divers. Then you move on to another location and see a lemon shark or a mako and . . ." She shrugged. "You see a ton of people who should know better than thrashing around in the water to get back to the boat."

"Don't I know it," he said, shaking his head.

"What? You're kidding me. You dive now, too?"

He laughed. "Spring break, first year of college. A group of us headed over to the Cayman Islands. We took quickie classes and then the real thing back at school. Love it. So far, you leave the world behind, unless you're a Navy Seal or the like, filming underwater maybe . . . but so far, you don't bring your cell phone down, and you leave the world behind except for your own bubbles and the beauty of the water and the nature around you."

"All that and you're still here!" Jessy said. "It sounds like you should have moved to the Florida Keys!"

"I do have a condo down there," he told her.

She laughed, her brows shooting up. "Cows to sea cows!"

"You got it!"

It was fun standing there, her hand on Bandit's head, laughing with the man she had known as a kid, finding out how strangely certain things in their lives had been on parallel lines.

"Well, remember me on that one! One day, when you're involved in a million business ventures, I'll be borrowing that condo!" she warned him.

"You got it," he told her.

"Okay, thanks! So, hmm. I really should—"

"Yeah, yeah, again, I didn't mean to hold you. Get on to your place, and anyway, I'm here if you need anything, if we can help you in any way. Oh! Wait! Hey, I'm playing tonight. If you're bored, if you want something to do. At the pub, starting about eight. And you're more than welcome to join us about six-thirty there for dinner first," he said.

She smiled and nodded, then frowned, grimacing. "That phenomenal education and talent—"

"Thanks, on that."

"And you aren't hitting the arenas?" she asked him. *Rude! she told herself silently, wincing at her own words. Accusing him of not bothering to use any of his potential.*

But he just smiled. "I love music. But I do have other interests in life. Yeah, local pub, but—"

"Oh, I am sorry! I didn't mean it that way. I mean—"

He laughed, interrupting her with, "City girl. Come on, this place isn't so bad. We're not that far from some amazing places. I love Colorado Springs and all kinds of places within the state here. You got a bunch of your big buildings in Denver, Boulder . . . I am a strangely happy man. Still living with my parents, you're thinking? No, I have my own little place on the property. And I do need to travel frequently on business now. But yes! I love my mom and dad and I love our cows—you gave me that, you know."

"What?" Jessy demanded, stunned that she might have had an effect on his life in any way.

"You looked like you were petting a pack of puppies that long-ago day."

"Did I turn you into a pescatarian?" she asked him.

He shrugged. "I still eat bacon. Pigs will eat a human being—I saw an interesting example in one of my college classes. But cows . . . Anyway, go! I hope to see you later!"

"Maybe!" she told him, giving Bandit one last pat and sliding back behind the steering wheel.

It didn't take a full five minutes to drive the rest of the way to her grandfather's property.

Her property now, she reminded herself with a wince.

And once she had come down the long drive past several of the pastures to the house, she saw that she had been expected.

The staff were all out to greet her.

Cody Connelly, rugged looking, fiftyish, weathered from years in the sun, but quick to smile—the ranch manager. He stood with Eddie Andrews, Tate Laughton, and David Benson, the men who worked with Cody to feed the animals, keep the stalls clean, work with the horses and customers as well. Eddie was only about thirty, the newest in the group, sandy-haired and boyish. Tate was closer to Cody's age and had been at the ranch for as long as Jessy could remember. He was tall and lean with his dark hair just beginning to show signs of gray. David Benson was just a few years younger than Cody and Tate, but his hair had already turned a silvery gray. He was a big man, stocky and strong.

And along with the ranch hands, she saw with a smile, Samantha Miller and Jenson Applegate were lined up to greet her as well. Samantha was also around fifty; a slim, wiry woman, always energetic, she had been a staple at the ranch since Jessy had been a child. Jenson looked just the way a business manager should look; he was dressed in a suit and might have walked out of any major corporation in New York City. A man of about forty, he appeared as if he could handle anything that had to do with function and paperwork. Dark hair cut short, he was about six feet even and fit. He'd been with the Danson ranch for about ten years.

"Sweetheart!"

It was Samantha who greeted her with such enthusiasm, stepping forward to give her a warm hug. "Of course, we miss your grampa terribly," Samantha told her, "but we're so very happy you're here!"

And next, of course, the dogs, Misty and Morgan, big sweet German shepherds who could almost bark louder than any alarm known to man. Her grandfather had always depended on them. They knew who belonged on the ranch and who didn't.

A chorus went up among all those around her, echoing Samantha's words, all the group welcoming her.

Welcoming her *home*.

She decided not to say anything about it not really being "home" at all at that time; it was just nice to greet people who had loved her grandfather and were truly happy to see her.

"It's wonderful to see all of you. And to thank you, for all that you did for my grandfather for so many years!"

"Working for your grandfather was a pleasure," Cody said.

"We'll get your things out of the car!" Eddie told her.

"I wasn't sure what room you wanted," Samantha told her, light blue eyes sparkling. "But you had your old room set up nicely last time you were here—" She broke off with a laugh, her powder-blue eyes bright. "You took down all your old boy-band crush posters, repainted, and your grampa bought those great drapes that matched the bedspread. And the room has a private bathroom, so I figured you could start off there. You can always change to a different room somewhere along the line if you wanted."

"No, that's great and fine; my old room is great. And—" Jessy began.

"Not to worry about your own work when you're here!" Eddie told her. "I've got the office set up for you, new computer, every art program known to man. I'm the youngest, so yeah, hey, the right one to take care of a computer situation. But you're a real artist, too, so I researched the best pencils, paints, all that . . . got a few easels and anything I could think of, and I honestly hope and believe I've covered everything you might need!"

"Oh, come on now!" Cody said. "Tate and David and I did a heck of a lot of the hauling!"

"Old people can haul well!" David said, making a face that caused them all to laugh.

"Thank you, thank you all!" she told them. "And please don't worry about supplies; I'm sure that everything is going to be great. And all is truly appreciated. You shouldn't have gone through so much trouble—"

"Well, they needed to, because I am going to need to hit you with all manner of business concerns almost immediately," Jenson told her apologetically. "Some silly, some more important. They've called from the Oak Tree Rodeo for one, wanting to know if you're going to be riding at the event, showcasing Danson Ranch."

"Oh, uh, well, I'm guessing one of you might want—"

"We're going to be participating in some of the events, but come on, Jessy!" Cody said. "You can show off a quarter horse better than anyone I know. Remember the fun riding you were doing last time you were here out with the barrels? I don't think I ever saw your grampa enjoy any spectacle more!"

She forced a smile and nodded. "Thanks!" she said softly. "Um, Jenson, please, give me just a few hours to get settled—"

"Of course. We'll just need answers on a few things by tomorrow," he told her.

"And I promise you I will have answers by tomorrow," Jessy promised. "So, for now—"

"Hey, guys! The poor girl has been driving for a while!

We'll all get you in and give you some peace!" Samantha promised. "We haven't let her in the house yet!"

Jessy smiled, nodding. Soon enough, she'd get to the stables to say her hellos to the horses. Right now, she just wanted to get a bit settled.

Cody laughed and offered her a hand, though, of course, it was nothing to head up the few wooden steps to the porch and the front door. But she smiled and took his hand.

Entering, she felt a wall of emotion. She had spent so much of her growing-up time here. The house wasn't elegant; it was *warm*. The floors were wooden, covered here and there with throw rugs in handsome designs, some depicting horses, some just colorfully designed with local flora and fauna.

Most were antique.

Like the furniture. It was Victorian, just like the house. And a massive fireplace was framed by an equally large mantel, filled with family pictures.

Her family, of course.

And of course, a curving stairway led to the second floor with its partial balcony overlooking the large parlor along with the hallways to the bedrooms.

She paused just inside the front door.

"Good to be back?" Samantha asked her. "I know you love New York. I love New York! I've only gotten to be there a few times, but . . . it is cool. But so is the ranch. Oh, well, it can be a beautiful world, cool things so many places. But . . . I can't tell you how much we miss your grandfather. No one could have been a better, kinder, more giving boss. But he was smart, too. Any one of us would have done anything in the world for him!"

"I get that; I adored him," Jessy murmured.

"Getting the luggage up!" Cody said, passing her with a suitcase.

David was right behind him, bringing her second bag. And Eddie and Tate were there, too. Eddie reminded her to check out the office and see if she liked the way he had fixed it up for her.

"I'm sure it's going to be wonderful!" she told him. "Thank you!"

"Oh, and I can get you just about anything in the world you might desire to eat or drink!" Samantha assured her. "I stocked the kitchen!"

She thanked everyone and ran up the steps to her room. She'd had her own room here as long as she could remember. Yes, it had changed over the years, reflecting her age. And it was set up for an adult now, and . . .

With everyone gone at last to get on with their own work, she threw herself back on her bed and stared up at the ceiling. She winced, thinking herself a horrible person. She should be the most grateful person alive. Yes, she had great parents, a great life as an adult, she loved her work, and . . .

She also had this, this incredible place filled with people who cared deeply about her, who had also been a part of her life. Even if her grandfather was now gone, all that he taught her, amazing memories, were here.

"Okay, I am horrible, I shouldn't be such a whining diva!" she told herself aloud, giving herself a mental shake. She still couldn't stay. New York City. The art, the museums, the nightlife, the music, so many wonderful friends, her folks!

Of course, she hoped her parents might well be out here soon enough!

She lay there, thinking that when she had her meeting with Jenson over the business discussion that he wanted, she'd have Cody there, too. She'd let them know she was putting management entirely in their hands. And yes, of course, she would come out as she had all her life to help with anything that she was really needed for, but . . .

She wouldn't be living there!

There was a tap on her door. She frowned, forcing herself to rise.

She was stunned to open her door and discover that Wyatt McFarlane was standing there. He appeared to have showered. His hair was still damp, slicked back on his head. He was still in jeans, a new denim shirt, and his denim jacket. She realized he smelled alluringly of soap, a shower, and aftershave. He grinned, arching a brow as she looked at him with surprise.

"Figured you might not come tonight if I didn't stop by to get you," he told her. He shrugged. "Okay, pressure you."

"Tonight? Um, well, I hadn't thought that much about it yet—"

"Good. I'll think for you! Grab your bag. I'll drive. It will be late when we're done with the gig, but hey, I'll get you home right after."

She smiled, but a warning light inside was going on.

No, he was being a friend, a neighbor, and it was far too easy for her to remember that she'd had her school-girl crush on him, but now he was a man, and she was all grown up, too!

But if she didn't go . . .

What was she going to do that night? Lie there and torture herself about the past and the future, the ranch and New York City?

"Oh, well, listen," she said lightly. "You actually smell good, and I haven't had a chance—"

"Plenty of time for you to hop in—I'll wait downstairs," he told her.

"I, uh . . ."

Well, she was here. And there was nothing wrong with dinner and music. And . . .

"Uh, okay."

He laughed. "I'll be downstairs," he told her.

"I'll be quick."

He left the room, and she could hear him talking to Samantha in the hall and then heading back downstairs.

She hadn't even opened her luggage yet, but she did so quickly. She pulled out a casual knit dress to wear—it was not a formal place, she'd been to the pub her last time here—and she thought it was fine for the atmosphere of the place.

She did tell herself that she was a little crazy, but she showered with the speed of light, hurriedly dressed, and walked on downstairs.

The house had a small formal dining room and something that was more like a larger but casual ban-quet area. The table there sat fourteen or fifteen people when necessary. As Jessy came down, she saw that Samantha—perhaps with help from one of the men—had made dinner for the group. Cody, Eddie, David, and Tate were seated with dinner on the table already.

Wyatt was sitting with them, chatting, enjoying a cup of coffee. But . . .

He'd been leaning low, smiling, yet Jessy had the odd feeling he was intent on whatever conversation was going on, maybe even intent on everyone in the room.

"And there she is! Our Miss America!" Cody said, seeing her and grinning. "Hey, Sam and I get to be very proud—we knew her since she was a wee babe!"

"Well, thank you, I don't know much about Miss America, but I am showered at any rate," Jessy said lightly.

"Well, it's great that you're getting out," Samantha told her.

She wondered if they'd been talking about her. Maybe knowing that she intended to leave.

Was that the reason Wyatt had seemed so intent? No. She couldn't have become that important so quickly.

"Yeah, and I'll be out there myself in a few hours!" Eddie said. "Wyatt's group is great! You'll see."

"I expect no less!" Jessy said, grinning at Wyatt.

"Then, we'll head out," Wyatt said. "Samantha, thanks for the coffee!"

"You got it. Have fun!" Samantha told them.

As Wyatt grinned at her and politely offered his arm, she wondered.

Maybe she would have fun.

Didn't mean that she was staying!

And . . .

Yes, she was attracted to Wyatt McFarlane. Chemistry? Did he have the same effect on everyone?

But there had been something odd about his being there, for her, after all this time. Naturally, as a friendly thing, he'd invited her to watch him play.

But coming here, to pick her up for the evening out? Sitting at the table with the ranch's staff, chatting as if just waiting for her, enjoying his cup of coffee?

There was something that seemed to be . . . off.

Something about it all seemed . . .

Suspicious!

But why on earth would it be?

CHAPTER 2

"So, I'm guessing that the crew was happy to see you, right?" Wyatt asked Jessy.

Of course he knew that they were. Jessy's commitment to the ranch meant their jobs.

She looked at him, arching a brow. "I think you've talked to everyone more than I've had a chance to. Looked like a good discussion was going on in the five minutes I took to shower."

He smiled. "You were fast, but that shower was ten minutes. And yeah, Sam offered me coffee, and it would have been rude not to accept and sit with them all. It's hard not to know people around here when you have the only homes fairly close to one another in a fair-sized sea of ranches."

"People—and cows and horses and a few other creatures," Jessy murmured.

"You do well with them, but the cows aren't really great conversationalists," he said dryly.

He looked ahead.

Wyatt knew he was good at what he did; he could

present almost any front, or personality, talk in the most casual way . . .

And most often, find out what he needed to know.

Not that he really suspected anyone at the Danson ranch could be guilty of what had been going on. But Jessy's arrival had been fortunate, allowing him an easier opportunity to slip in where he needed to be.

And it wasn't as if he was simply taking advantage of an old friend. He had always really liked Jessy; she'd been an amazingly cool kid. But yes, Jessy's arrival was opportune. Of course, it seemed like he hadn't seen her in forever. It had been several years. And he did know all about her and her work—she had been her grampa's pride and joy. Wyatt really had purchased books where she had been credited as the visual artist or paper engineer.

She was talented. Confident, he could see, and a truly beautiful young woman. She had a headful of golden hair that hadn't darkened a bit since she'd been a child. It waved down the length of her back. Art was her world, he knew, and he smiled inwardly. Speaking of greats—her face might have been sculpted by one of the great sculptors. She had high cheekbones, large amber eyes—truly not brown or green, but a unique amber—and full, perfectly formed lips. She was both lean and shapely.

Yeah, the kid had grown up, all right!

"You come to hang out with Sam, Cody, and the crew often?" she asked.

"Cody has been at the council meetings for the rodeo next weekend, and a few of the others have shown up with him now and then," Wyatt said. "Samantha—as much as she's always loved the ranch and working for your grandfather and now for you, I'm sure—isn't a fan. She once said she thought bull riding was one of the most stupid exercises in dangerous sports she'd ever seen. And for all her years at a horse ranch, she doesn't ride. So, she doesn't take part in any way. Oh, except she says that she did take nursing and critical care classes so she could patch up anyone in the household when necessary."

"It's always good to have that support on the sidelines," Jessy said. She was looking forward, but he knew that at times, she was looking at him curiously, too.

Well, of course. She knew what he'd been up to over the years, just as he knew what she had been doing. Except she didn't know what he had really been doing at all.

Few people did.

"Will you ride?" he asked her.

She shrugged. "Maybe. I . . ." She hesitated and shrugged. "It's not like I have a timeline, and I haven't told the household yet, but I can't really live out here."

"Can't—or won't?"

She didn't answer for a minute and then she looked at him and said, "If my dad hadn't been ill, the place should have and could have gone straight to him. And he's doing great in recovery, but I don't really want to be more than half the country away from him while he *is* in recovery. And . . ."

"You spent most of your time growing up in the city and you're a city girl," he offered.

She laughed. "City girl. Out here, you know, that's an insult!"

"Not an insult. Rather a state of mind," he told her.

"I do love the ranch. And I loved my grandfather—"

"I don't know a soul who didn't," Wyatt assured her. Beyond a doubt, at least that was true.

She smiled. "Yeah, he was a good guy. The best. And my dad is just like him, except that his expertise was in technology at a time when few people knew everything that he did. And he had such a great future in the city. Oh! You know, my grandfather encouraged him to take the job with the tech company that he's had since he was in his twenties. My grandfather wanted people to be happy, to do what they wanted to do . . ."

Her words trailed and she appeared to be frowning. And he thought that he might understand.

"Did he put pressure on *you* to come back here?"

She shrugged and nodded. "And it's not as if I don't love the place!"

"Hey, I love it, too, but I'm gone as much as I'm here. Work," he explained briefly. "You never know. Just keep the old place going. Then maybe someday you'll have kids. And while you may raise them in New York City, they'll discover that they want to own and manage a quarter horse ranch. Maybe your grandfather just wanted to make sure his beloved land stayed in the family," Wyatt offered.

"Right. I don't plan on letting the place go," Jessy told him.

He laughed. "That's a relief."

"Well, I'm glad you're glad," she told him, smiling.

"It's so hard to break in new neighbors!" he said lightly.

Being with her . . . it was an oddly nice perk.

But then, of course, she asked, "Work? You're gone a lot for work? I thought your family's ranch was your work!"

"Um, no, I work with a studio in the city," he told her. It was semi-true.

"Music! Of course. I'm so glad you're keeping up with it. I mean, I'm not knocking the pub tonight, it's just I'm glad that you're putting it all to use often!"

"When you love music, you love music."

"I love music. I just don't have your talent."

"Are you kidding me? First, you do have musical talent. I remember you working with camp choruses and the way your family loved to go around in the city at Christmastime doing carols! That's just music. Your art—and your paper engineering—is fantastic!"

"Thank you."

"And you can be an artist anywhere, you know."

She grinned. "I know. I've heard that from my dad— and even my mom—my whole life."

"Your mom aways loved this place, from what I can remember," he said.

Jessy nodded. "But my dad is really something of a tech genius. He's helped with many medical improvements. I mean, Mom teaches grade school; and I know she could teach anywhere, too. But with my dad . . . they both thought it was important that he worked where he worked. My mom agreed, and . . . well, there you go. I'm a New York kid."

"I'll just remind you that art can be created anywhere, and then I'll shut up on it," he promised, "and just hope that you have a good time tonight. Tad is on drums tonight and I think you know his wife, Marci, don't you?" he asked her.

She smiled. "I do. Marci is just a year older than me. We took some of our barrel racing lessons together when we were kids."

"She'll be there. And other nice people, I promise."

"I'd expect no less!" she teased.

They arrived at the pub in another five minutes. Tad Clifton and Marci were already there, along with Brett Marshall, bassist, and Josh Percy, on keyboards that night. Marci greeted Jessy with enthusiasm, then extended her condolences, and then told her again how happy she was to see her. Brett Marshall's girlfriend, Casey Larkin, was there as well. And soon everyone was talking as the owner—a true Irishman named Brian Murphy, grandson of the original Murphy— welcomed them all cheerfully and gave them their seats at a large table in the back. He told Wyatt happily that he had several dozen reservations for the night—locals and visitors to the Colorado Springs area as well.

"They all heard the Rustic Cowboys were playing!" Brian told them, beaming.

Brian was a nice guy, in his early forties now, tall, with a headful of rich red hair that had come down through generations.

Wyatt was surprised to feel a sting of jealousy when

the man greeted Jessy with a warm hug that seemed to offer a great deal of genuine affection.

He gave himself a mental swat.

Sure, Jessy Danson was an old childhood friend; it was good to see her. But she wasn't staying, and it was foolish to appreciate the beautiful woman she had grown to be when she was going to leave the area. It was, of course, nice to see a nice human being, and he almost felt guilty about using her, except that . . .

No matter what had been going on, he would have asked her here tonight just because she was an old friend!

Maybe the night would be fun, despite what was going on.

They sat, chatted, ordered—salmon for Jessy, and he decided on it himself. And then, maybe naturally, the conversation turned to the strange spate of robberies— and worse—that had been going on.

"I mean, yeah," Tad said. "Sadly, it's almost Christmas, so things start to happen. I mean, sometimes, someone is desperate. There's a charity collection pail, and a man or woman starving on the tracks decides they've got to eat. That I get—and a night in jail does pay for a meal. But these robberies! And a couple of nights ago, someone got really hurt—she's in intensive care. And a girl was kidnapped! At Christmas."

New York obviously had its own share of crime, but Jessy's look of confusion proved she hadn't heard about the case.

"What's going on?" she asked worriedly.

"Weird robberies," Brett explained, shaking his

head. "The first one—no one really noticed. A house was broken into in Denver, every Christmas present waiting under the tree was stolen along with jewelry, technology, the usual—but then the Christmas tree was slashed up as if someone hated Christmas. No forensics—that's what they say in the papers, anyway. Thieves are wearing gloves. They knock out any surveillance cameras. And there are so many people going around now, carolers, church representatives, solicitors . . . there hasn't been anything like a reliable witness yet!"

"Right, but you're not explaining it all, Brett!" Casey told him. "Okay, happens in Denver, Boulder, and then Colorado Springs. Then they realize it started in the four corners region where Colorado, New Mexico, Arizona, and Utah meet. The robbers hit a home in each state, and, of course, with all those states, different police and law enforcement are called in on it. So you wind up with the federal government and the FBI as main control on the case," she told Jessy.

"Wow," Jessy murmured. "That's . . . sad!"

"But that's not the half of it," Marci said. "First, no one was home, no one got hurt. Then, an elderly man is home when they break in; he gets a paper bag from his own kitchen thrown over his head, and he's forced into a closet where he's locked in with a chair pressed against the knob. Guy winds up in the hospital with a cardiac arrest—luckily, law enforcement saved him."

"There's a Christmas present for you," Tad murmured. "At least he's alive!"

"They know this is all the same person—or persons, I guess?" Jessy asked.

"Or persons," Wyatt said. It might seem strange if he didn't get in on the conversation. He shrugged. "The number of things they're taking, the way they're managing to avoid cameras, get in, get out . . . they think that there are probably two to three people in on it."

That information was in the newspapers.

"But what happened a few nights ago? A girl was kidnapped, you said. Someone was hurt—where, where did this happen?" Jessy asked, concerned.

"Colorado Springs, the third event to take place there or in the surrounding area," Tad said.

"But what happened?" Jessy asked, her beautiful eyes wide, her face a mask of concern. Concern—empathy, Wyatt thought. And that was nice. She wasn't anxious for herself—and with the number of people working and living at the Danson ranch and at his own home, he didn't believe the thieves would try to strike there. No, her feelings were for others. And that was nice.

That was the way her family was. That was the way she had been taught, and still . . . complete kindness was part of the human soul as well.

Whoa, boy, he told himself. *Major-league events on the horizon; no time for a crush.*

"They broke in, the mom was knocked out cold in the kitchen, struck so hard her skull was fractured, and she's lucky to be alive. And a daughter, who just celebrated her eighteenth birthday, was taken out of the house," Marci told Jessy somberly. "No sign of her yet."

"They're sure the young woman was kidnapped or

forced out? Maybe she was gone for the night, visiting friends—" Jessy suggested.

Something law enforcement had investigated imme-diately, of course.

"Obviously, they checked that all out," Wyatt said, wincing as he spoke. The question had made him defen-sive; he was usually far more careful.

Thankfully, Marci jumped back in again. "They checked everything! Everyone she knew, everywhere she went . . . she was last seen in her afternoon class at the local junior college, and she told friends she was heading home to help her mother make cupcakes for a friend's bridal shower. Her car, just like her parents' cars, was found in front of the house. I mean, I guess I've gotten a little obsessed with reading about it all, but it's gotten too close!"

Yes, too close. Almost as if the distance from Colorado Springs at first had been a calculated plan, throwing everyone off.

"The corned beef and cabbage here is great!" Tad told Brian Murphy as he swept by to check on their table.

"Good. My dad used to tell me that in Ireland, his family had bacon and cabbage all the time—I guess different than the links we're accustomed to here. Maybe more like Canadian bacon. Whatever, I'm glad you're enjoying your dinner!" Brian said. "And . . ."

"Yeah, yeah, we're ready to go up, right?" Wyatt said, looking around the table. The members of the band nodded, and they stood, heading for the stage.

"Go, Rustic Cowboys!" Jessy said lightly.

Wyatt smiled back at her. "You'll get yours!" he promised.

They had a "pub set" that they all knew and loved, not because they had so many chances to practice or jam together these days as they'd once had, but through the years they'd gotten good with several Christmas songs as well. But they started with one of their own creations, "Cows, Cowboys, and Christmas and a Kinda Christmas Carol," and thankfully, their audience seemed to enjoy it tremendously. They moved into classic rock, tunes by the Eagles, the Stones, Queen, and then took it into country for a few minutes before switching back into Christmas carols.

That's when Wyatt looked at Jessy and announced they had a guest singer joining them that night, joining them from out of state and far, far away, but that she was glad to be here—a place that was almost something like home.

Jessy stared at him in shock, shaking her head, but Marci was literally pushing her up, and the others at the table were encouraging her as well.

And he couldn't help himself. They'd met as children.

"I dare ya—double dare ya!" he mouthed to her.

A minute later, she gave in, glaring at him.

"Artist, not a musician!" she reminded him softly as Tad drew up a mic for her.

"But this was your grandfather's favorite carol of all time!" he reminded her. "And we're in an Irish pub!"

She almost smiled.

"We did this together when we were kids for our

families—not always that thrilled they put us together!" he said, grinning at her.

He realized his words were true. There was a lot of history between them he hadn't realized until now. He'd been older, she'd been a "child" in his eyes at that time when three or four years was a major difference. But her grandfather and parents had been close with his parents, and so they'd been thrown together.

Maybe she was thinking the same thing because she had an answer for him!

"Oh! You were just older and cooler—annoyingly!" she announced, which brought them a spate of laughter. And then he began with the lead guitar and the band joined him.

And after the intro, Jessy easily fell into a rendition of "What Child Is This?" with him, the beautiful song her grandfather had loved so very much, a Christmas carol to the tune of "Greensleeves."

She almost smiled at him with warmth and meaning.

And their song was greeted with more thunderous applause than they had received yet, and along with it, he could see some people telling each other that in a way she was a local girl, the granddaughter of Kelly Danson, returned to take over the Danson ranch.

Of course, there were tourists who had just wandered in and had no idea who Jessy was, other than a lovely young woman.

On the one hand, the night was great. Jessy seemed to have a good time and people seemed to love her— those who knew her as well as those who didn't.

But he hated what he was doing.

No! He would have invited her tonight no matter what. And they had sung the song together before, when they were kids making their elders happy.

But even before Jessy had gotten here, he'd been in a war with himself. His boss was certain that someone local was involved—or perhaps all those who were involved were local.

He didn't believe it for a minute. He knew his neighbors; he knew his bandmates. And he and the Rustic Cowboys had accepted this invitation from Brian Murphy long ago, before the robberies had even become connected. But it was a way to discover where everyone had been and when they'd been there.

Same with hands and staff at his family's ranch, just as it had been with Jessy's family ranch.

And so far . . . nothing.

Then again, at Murphy's Pub, he was able to see several of the people who were "outskirts" citizens, those living right on the edges of Colorado Springs, or perhaps between that area and another bigger city.

And he understood the urgency.

These criminals had either become hardened somewhere or watched too much TV. They knew all about security cameras, traffic cams, gloves, and masks.

He wasn't in the best position. The Colorado Springs office hadn't pulled in agents until the attacks had begun here, which meant they hadn't seen any of the initial crime scenes or been in at the start when it came to forensics or witness descriptions.

But Christmas was on the horizon. And a young woman was missing. And Wyatt's superiors seemed to believe that no one knew the outskirts the way he did, and possibly someone he knew might be in on it all.

He'd known all his life what he had wanted to do. Yes, he loved music. He loved his family's ranch, and probably because of Jessy, he loved the fact that they raised dairy cows.

He kept his smile going. His band frontman persona in place.

As all things did, the night finally came to an end.

From the stage he thanked Jessy again for having joined them, and he introduced each of his band members.

Of course, when it was time to go, Marci and his bandmates all wanted hugs again from Jessy, telling her how great it was to have her, and hoping, hoping, they'd get together more often now that she was there.

Jessy just smiled at them all, agreed it had been great to be together, and remained completely noncommittal about where she would be when.

Then they were in the car again on the way home. She was quiet, staring ahead.

He glanced at her quickly as he drove.

"So, sorry, yeah, everyone wishes that you were staying. But it's okay, you don't need to be worried or depressed about it or—"

"No!" she protested. "I wasn't thinking about that at all."

"What were you thinking about?"

"A girl, missing, when Christmas is just days away. Folks in the hospital, trying to get better—but I heard about it all, and . . . well, how do you get better when your child is missing?"

"Trust me, it's weighing on me. And cops and agents, too, I'm sure."

She looked at him. "Their home was right outside Colorado Springs?"

"Yes."

"Not far from here."

"Probably about a thirty-minute drive. Colorado Springs is about forty-five minutes in rush hour, and yeah, there can be something of a rush hour."

He was surprised when she set a hand on his arm. Good thing he was a steady driver; her touch was a bit of a shock.

"I want to go there."

"Jessy, there's crime scene tape on the house, I'm certain. And if there wasn't, we couldn't just break into someone's house," he told her, confused that she had said such a thing.

"No, I don't want to break into the house. I didn't mean the house. I meant the area. Okay, taking this girl wasn't in their usual plan. I don't think that they took her far away to kill her or leave her body in an alley—or in a cow pasture—anywhere. She's going to be near that house. I mean, if it's a bit on the outskirts, they may have outbuildings beyond the home—or homes—in the area. Wyatt, on our property, there's an old shed back in the trees that is never used now; they built a new one closer to the stables years ago. Please, I know this is crazy. I know it's nearly two in the morning, but I have a feeling that she's there, near there, somewhere!"

"Hey, you're the one who has a meeting at the crack of dawn," he reminded her.

"Not crack of dawn; we don't have a set time. And we can be back by four, and I've gone on four hours of sleep before!" she said, her tone entreating.

"I . . . uh, okay. But we don't do anything that will get us arrested!"

"No, we'll just go through any fields, check out any old outbuildings, okay?"

"Well, it is trespassing to crawl around on other people's land," he reminded her.

"People get out of their cars and walk on other people's land all the time around here. They don't always know what's embankment, state land, whatever!"

"Fences usually indicate that a property is owned."

"Dammit! Fine. I'll get a car at my ranch and do it myself!"

"No! I didn't say I wouldn't do it," he told her.

What the hell! He was the undercover agent. She was determined that they work a case she'd just heard about that night!

So much for worrying about his growing feelings of attraction and romance! She was on the hunt—and he definitely did not want her going home to get her rental car or borrow someone else's! He couldn't believe himself that those he had known for years could be guilty of any of this.

But he didn't *know. He just didn't know!*

And he sure as hell wasn't going to put her into any danger.

"Fine! Look up the exact address. Some reporter got wind of it, and the address where the attack and the robbery took place is online somewhere."

"Gotcha," she told him, pulling out her phone.

It took her a few minutes to find the right article. That didn't really matter; he knew exactly where the house was, and he drove in the right direction while she searched.

And he'd been right. It took him just about thirty minutes to reach the property.

It wasn't just a house, but it wasn't a large ranch, either. The home sat on about five acres with woods abutting the rear of the property. There were old stables and a tack room to the right of the front entry, but they'd been searched; he knew that because he'd been there.

A beautifully manicured lawn took up the front of the house, and there were still pastures to the right and left of the main house.

But there was also a large stretch of forested state land to the right of the entry.

He pulled off the road, staring into the trees by night.

"You know, a satellite image of this area might be helpful. I know some local law enforcement—"

"And if she's been back there for almost two days now, she might not make it until morning!" Jessy said.

True.

He exited the car. "Well . . ."

It could be damned dark at night. Sure, homes out here might be decked out with Christmas lights, but they were few and far between.

"We have our phones for light," she said, as if reading his thoughts.

"Yeah, and hang on. I have a major-league flashlight in the trunk."

He did, of course. He pulled it out and saw that there

was a trail through the trees, overgrown, old, probably not used much these days . . .

But there were some broken branches he could see once he'd pulled out his light, and it was more than possible that someone had been through there lately.

"Stay behind me!" he snapped.

She did, apparently glad he had a light and now seemed as determined as she was.

"You do know," he reminded her, "that we have more than just criminal human beings roaming around these parts. They've had a few animal attacks on cattle and sheep lately, too. Coyotes, wolves, black bears, mountain lions . . . just to name a few."

"So, we should probably hurry then!" she told him.

He kept walking, pausing now and then to listen.

But he didn't hear any twigs snapping or any rustle of leaves that might indicate a predator was in the woods ready to prowl after them.

"What are you doing?" she asked when he stopped once.

"Listening. Did you forget everything about the weeks each year you did spend growing up out here?" he asked her.

"Right. Sorry."

He stopped again, listening, certain he had heard something . . .

But not a predator. Not a dangerous creature coming through the woods for them.

He thought he heard . . . crying.

"What is it?" Jessy whispered.

"Listen!" he told her.

They both stood very still.

And it came again. So soft it was almost like the whisper of a breeze.

"I hear it!" Jessy cried.

She tried to push past him; he stopped her.

"I still go first!"

"Listen, I'm honestly tough for a girl—"

"No, I go first because I live out here and you don't!" he snapped.

And he was moving forward, pausing again where there seemed to be a fork in the almost nonexistent trail, throwing his light on the bushes and trees, determining where twigs might have fallen, where branches might have broken.

To the left.

Then he paused again, lifting a hand. And she understood. They were both listening.

Nothing.

But he moved ahead, shining his light far beyond them.

Nothing.

Except . . .

They'd come to a small clearing, a very small clearing, just about eight feet by eight feet had the area been a square. And there were branches on the ground, leaves . . . too many of them, Wyatt thought.

"I heard it!" Jessy said, her voice distressed and frustrated. "I know I heard someone crying, barely, crying, but . . . sniffles, something!"

"Yes. I heard it, too," Wyatt said.

He looked at the ground again. It was wrong. Just wrong.

He fell to his knees and began to push and shove at the branches, lifting the bigger ones and throwing them back into the trees.

In seconds, Jessy was on her knees at his side, busily doing the same thing.

He might be foolish, working at nothing.

But he'd heard the sound, too. Someone was out here somewhere. And . . .

Right when he was ready to despair, he hit something that wasn't the hard ground. In fact, it made a noise, too, a knocking sound, and he hit it again and again and . . .

Wood. It had to be a hatch cover to some old hole in the earth, maybe even a bomb shelter built during the years of the Cold War or some such thing.

"Wyatt! It's a—a lid or something!" Jessy cried.

"Right. Keep moving the dirt and all . . . there's got to be a latch, something that pulls it up, somewhere, under all this!"

"On it!"

And she was. Working hard and getting her hands— well, all of her—dirty didn't seem to be anything that held her back or bothered her in any way.

They both worked feverishly. It had to be only seconds.

Then he found it. His fingers lit on an old metal latch, and he inched back, allowing himself to get a good grip on the thing.

"Yes, yes, oh, my God, yes!" Jessy breathed.

He pulled at the latch and the wooden cover gave

easily, opening to allow them to see downward into a stygian darkness.

He grabbed the light that he had left on the ground to allow them to move the dirt, leaves, and branches aside.

He cast its brilliant strength down into the hole.

A ladder led downward about twenty feet. Beyond that . . .

"Hello!" Jessy called. "Are you in there? We're here to help you." She looked at Wyatt.

"Chrissie. Her name is Chrissie Dunworth."

She gave her attention to the hole. "Chrissie! Are you down there?"

There was no reply. Wyatt handed the light to Jessy and maneuvered himself onto the ladder. He headed down as quickly as he could.

"Toss me the light!" he told Jessy.

Of course, it was Jessy. She didn't toss it to him; she carried it down the ladder.

Whatever it had been once, it was just a big hole in the earth now.

"My God!" Jessy breathed.

And she dropped the light on the floor, running the few steps to the rear of the hole. Wyatt had his phone out, dialing 911.

Because there was a young woman there, passed out now—or worse—against the dirt at the far side of the underground hole.

He'd heard her before, heard her whimpering!

She'd been alive just moments before . . .

She wasn't moving; she wasn't whimpering anymore.

He could only pray for a Christmas miracle.

CHAPTER 3

Chrissie Dunworth—oh so thankfully—had a pulse. It was weak, but it was there, almost steady. And she was breathing, just nonresponsive. Still, Jessy had tremendous hope she'd be all right; she'd let out sounds just moments before.

"We shouldn't move her, right?" she asked Wyatt.

"Probably safest if we wait for those who are trained. I doubt she's broken any bones. I think she was terrified, dehydrated by now, and starving. But . . . I hear the sirens already!" he said. "Stay with her; I'll leave that light. I want to make sure that the EMTs find us."

He hurried back up the ladder. When he did so, Chrissie stirred.

Then her eyes opened, and she stared at Jessy.

Before she could scream, Jessy spoke to her. "It's all right, it's all right. Medical folks are on their way, and you're going to go into the hospital to get checked out. You're safe; we're getting you help!"

Giant tears filled the girl's eyes.

"Thank you!" she whispered. "My mom, my dad—"

"They're at the hospital."

"But my mom is—"

"Alive. She's alive. And from everything I've read and heard, Chrissie, your dad has been with your mom at the hospital while making sure everyone kept searching for you."

"You're a cop?" Chrissie asked.

"I, uh, no. I'm an artist, but my grandfather just left me property near here that isn't unlike this . . . well, we didn't have underground storage and I was just looking for old outbuildings, but my friend and I both heard you . . . and we're going to get you to the hospital. Your mom and dad will be able to see you! They'll be so happy, Chrissie, so hang in there. You need to hang in there—"

The girl almost smiled.

"You're an artist?"

Jessy managed to smile in return.

"Yep. Just out here because I have paperwork to sign. My grandfather was a super guy, and he just passed and . . ." Jessy stopped speaking with a shrug, wishing she had more medical training. Should she shut up and insist that the girl rest and save her breath, or was it good to keep her talking, awake and aware?

"Mainly kids' books!" Jessy said.

Chrissie smiled, but then a look of fear darkened her brow as she whispered, "They're gone? They're really gone? I guess they left me here to die, but they aren't out there, right? I mean, you're certain, they're not out there?"

"Long gone, Chrissie," she assured the girl. "I'm Jessy, by the way. Jessy Danson."

"Jessy!" Her name was called loudly from just above her; Wyatt was back.

Jessy wasn't sure how Wyatt had managed it, but he already had the EMTs at the hole in the ground. And in this situation, she was glad to see that the EMTs were young, strapping men. No matter how good one might be in emergency medicine, getting the young woman up a ladder and out of the hole wouldn't be an easy task.

But the two EMTs were already talking with Wyatt, and they had it figured it out. They'd gotten a litter down and were ready to slide Chrissie onto it when the girl started to cry, grasping Jessy's hand.

"Don't leave me, don't leave me!" she begged.

"I will not leave you; I will be right with you, I promise," Jessy told her. "But they must get you out of here. And Wyatt is my very good friend; I've known him all my life. He's going to be with you, too. He's the one who really found you!"

Wyatt spoke gently to Chrissie as well. He promised that Jessy would, indeed, be allowed to go with her all the way to the hospital. And neither of them would leave her until they knew she was all right, and they would stay until her father was with her.

"Chrissie, do you know who did this to you? Can you tell us anything?"

She shook her head. "I ran into the kitchen because I heard a thump! It was . . . it was my mom falling. My mom . . ."

"She's in the hospital, Chrissie, holding her own," Wyatt assured the young woman. "So, you heard the thump. You went into the kitchen and—"

"There was a feed bag thrown over my head, and I was thrown down on the floor, tied up and then . . . I heard them tearing the house apart, and then dragging me out, lifting me . . . I think that there were two of them. I mean, it was at least two, but . . ."

"You didn't see anything, see their faces?" Wyatt asked.

"No! I'm so sorry!"

"Chrissie, you don't need to be sorry about anything at all. But if you do think of anything, anything at all, something special in their voices, a tattoo on a wrist, anything, please, please, make sure the law enforcement officers and agents get to know!" Wyatt told her.

"Just don't leave me!"

"Jessy will be with you all the way," Wyatt promised her, looking at Jessy.

She nodded.

Of course!

Chrissie allowed herself to be put on the litter, and Jessy had to marvel at the way the three men manipulated the move. One of the EMTs got to the top and out of the hole while Wyatt followed him, grasping the front of the litter while the last man held the bottom. Then the EMT who was out of the hole grasped the top, and the two others fed him the length of the litter and emerged behind it. Jessy quickly followed them.

They hurried back through the path in the woods. An ambulance was parked behind Wyatt's car, but Chrissie started to cry again and begged Jessy to go with her.

She shrugged to Wyatt, and he nodded; he knew that she would do it. She hopped into the ambulance and held Chrissie's hand while one of the young EMTs started an IV to rehydrate the girl, speaking with the doctor who would meet them in the emergency room.

She was asked to wait outside as Chrissie was whisked into a room. Trying to calm herself down, she determined that she needed to be in the waiting room.

When she walked in, she discovered Wyatt was already there with a man of about forty-five, standing there unashamedly, tears running down his cheeks.

"That's her?" the man demanded of Wyatt.

"Yes, that's Jessy Danson," Wyatt said. "Sir—"

In a split second, the man was across the room, enveloping her in a hug, then stepping back apologetically, mumbling so that she could barely understand.

But she knew that the man had to be Chrissie's father.

"Sir, sir, it's all right. We're so grateful Chrissie is all right. And I know they'll let you see her soon—"

"Never, never in a thousand years on earth, could we thank you enough!" the man exclaimed. "And I'm sorry, I'm so, so sorry! I never understood—they could have had anything I owned, stolen everything, and it wouldn't have mattered. But my wife . . . they must keep her, make sure her brain doesn't bleed . . . and my daughter! But—"

"I truly believe your daughter will be fine!" Jessy told him, setting a hand on his shoulder. "And I have a lot of faith! I believe your wife will come out of it, too."

Maybe she shouldn't have spoken. She had no idea of what the condition of his wife might be, but he was so emotional, she felt she had to be reassuring.

She looked across the room, thinking Wyatt might step in and help her. But she frowned; Wyatt was out in the hallway.

There were officers there, police officers in uniform, and there were several people in regular clothing as well.

The feds had been given the lead in the investigations—straddling state lines—she had learned during dinner.

And they were all questioning Wyatt, who seemed to be gravely answering their questions. He pointed at her; she smiled grimly and a little hopelessly. She was still trying to help Mr. Dunworth.

Then a nurse came into the room, bright and happy, seeking Mr. Dunworth. He could come in and see his daughter. She was dehydrated, but they didn't think she'd need to stay more than the next day or perhaps the night just to ensure she was hydrated and suffering no other possible dangers from her strange captivity.

In fact, they could put her in a room with her mother—who still needed to be observed to ensure her health before she left the hospital.

Dunworth hugged Jessy fiercely again.

She smiled and dared to tease, "You need to hug my friend Wyatt McFarlane. I was looking for an outbuilding; Wyatt knew that there often were storage facilities underground!"

He smiled at her and nodded.

"I owe both of you my life!" he said.

She didn't get to reply. He hurried out of the room after the nurse, anxious to see his daughter. As he did so, the group beyond the waiting room windows broke apart and a dignified-looking man, with crew-cut silver hair, and a slightly younger woman joined Wyatt to come into the waiting room to talk with her.

"Jessy, these are Special Agents Mary Richter and Andy Soloman," Wyatt told her. "I'm afraid the night is going to get longer."

"Technically," Mary Richter said, grimacing as she looked at Jessy, "the morning is going to get much longer. And we apologize profusely, but we need you at our office in Colorado Springs. Paperwork. And forgive me, we're also horribly embarrassed! We thought we'd searched and searched and searched, looked forever and ever for any possible building. We're still unbelievably stunned and grateful that you happened to be in the state—and happened to be so determined to find the young lady!"

Jessy glanced at Wyatt. "Mary and my mom went to school together," he said. "She's great with paperwork. She'll be gentle!" he teased.

"But you—" she began.

"Oh, I'll be there. Paperwork for all of us," he said.

She was wondering if she'd feel like she was under arrest, but it wasn't that complicated. Wyatt was able to get his car so that the two of them could drive together.

"Jessy," he told her in the car, "you're amazing. There were dozens of people, local, federal, volunteers . . . all looking for that girl. And you were determined, and you found her!"

"Technically, you found her," Jessy said. She looked at Wyatt. He appeared to be distressed, almost angry with himself.

But not with her.

"Well, I just . . ." She paused, shaking her head, offering him a weak smile. "Wyatt, it's almost Christmas. But honestly, I think it was just knowing there were abandoned buildings on our property, some of them invisible because they are tangled in the trees. Because . . . well, we're not old out here like they are on the East Coast, but . . . there was a ranch on my granddad's property long before my family was there and . . ."

"You saved her life."

"If I did, I'm grateful. I still say you saved her life. I wouldn't have thought beneath the ground!"

"But I wouldn't have gone out there tonight if it hadn't been for you," he said softly.

"Well, we did go out there. And . . ."

Her phone was ringing. She winced. She hadn't thought to call anyone at the ranch to tell them what was happening.

"I'm awful—" she murmured.

"No, no, you're fine. I called Cody and told him where we were," Wyatt told her.

"Then—"

She looked at her phone. It was her mother.

"No, oh, no . . ." she whispered.

Wyatt glanced at her, frowning. She glanced back at him. She felt frozen.

What if her father had taken a turn for the worse? What if her father . . .

"I can take it for you, but, Jessy, you need to answer your mom."

"It's the crack of dawn!"

"Not back East. And she might have forgotten."

Jessy answered the call. "Mom?"

"Oh, honey, I'm so sorry!" her mother said. "I was so excited I forgot the time difference. Your dad is great! He's been cleared! We're going to come to you! The doctor just this second came out and . . . wow, right. I am sorry, darling. It's just after eight a.m. here, and I now realize you're on mountain time so it's just after six a.m. there. But your dad had the first appointment of the day, the eight a.m. appointment, and he's already out of his wheelchair and he's doing great, and he's cleared to fly! He hated you having to go out there without him, without us; but we're going to be on our way the day after tomorrow—we'll be there for Christmas Eve and Christmas. Of course, we'll miss your grandfather, but he'd be so happy we will all be out there, together, a family, loving the place as he did!"

Jessy swallowed hard. She'd been so afraid.

Christmas—out here?

Just as it had been for so, so many years!

And did it matter? She was so lucky. Her father was going to be all right!

She smiled and glanced at Wyatt.

"Mom, that's wonderful!" she said.

"I didn't mean to wake you," her mother said.

"Um, you didn't wake me. I was awake. And Mom, I'm so delighted! Make sure I get the time of your flight, and I'll be out to pick you up at the airport. Love you, love you. Tell Dad how grateful I am, how relieved."

Wyatt smiled at her.

"So, your dad is okay?" he asked.

She nodded, tears stinging her eyes. "I was so afraid!

I mean, grateful that a life had been saved, and then terrified because I might have lost . . . my dad. And I'm thinking now that I'm so selfish. My dad's condition didn't change the fact that Chrissie Dunworth is just eighteen, a girl who deserves a life—"

"Jessy! You're not being selfish at all. It's natural that you should love your father and worry about him, especially after just losing his father! Jessy, trust me, we're all human!"

He was so sweetly passionate as he spoke to her, so caring.

She accepted his words, nodding.

"Is it really six a.m.?" she asked him.

"Oh, yeah. But I did make calls and let them, and Cody, know you were all right. We just wound up being involved in a criminal case—in a good way," Wyatt said. "So, paperwork, and then home."

They reached the offices in Colorado Springs.

It was strangely . . . comfortable.

Wyatt seemed to know everyone there. He explained to her that several agents had grown up in the area, they'd known his parents, or someone who had worked at the ranch.

She answered questions.

She signed a statement.

Again, she received thanks from people who all seemed to want to kick themselves—they were agents.

In their minds, they'd failed while she—an unwilling visitor to the area, an artist, not trained in any way, shape, or form as an investigator—had found the kidnapped girl.

They had not.

But no one seemed angry at her in any way.

They were all just awed and grateful, Mary Richter assured her.

By the time they were done, it was nearly nine a.m., and she wondered if—especially since her parents would now be here the following day—she shouldn't just put her meeting with Jenson Applegate off a day.

As they left the offices in Colorado Springs and drove out to their ranches, she leaned back against the headrest and closed her eyes.

"You okay?" he asked.

"Yeah, fine. Of course. I'm just . . . exhausted. And when I get home, I'm going to go to sleep and deal with anything and everything tomorrow!"

"Good idea," he told her.

She opened her eyes and glanced at him. He was grinning.

"What?"

"You said the word *home.* You said, 'And when I get home—'"

"Oh, come on! Not fair. Okay, when you get me back to where I'm sleeping!" she said. She frowned and sat straight, glancing at him. "You know, I just realized how bad this whole thing really is! What, these guys have hit like six or seven times now? People weren't hurt at first, things were just stolen, but Chrissie could have died!"

"She could have." He shook his head. "I still can't

believe you insisted we get out there. So many people searched—"

"How do you know that?" she asked him. "Are you sure? Maybe it didn't even occur to anyone! If wouldn't be that strange if they assumed the kidnappers had taken her somewhere far from her home."

"Well, as it came up at dinner tonight, this has all been in the news several weeks now. And because Mrs. Dunworth wound up in the hospital and Chrissie was kidnapped, people are always talking about it," Wyatt said. "So, will you do me a favor?" he asked her.

"Of course," she told him.

"I can't help but be a little worried about you," he said. "Will you call me later and let me know that you're doing okay?"

She smiled. "Wyatt, I'll be doing fine. I'm not the one who was kidnapped."

"But you're worried."

"I'm worried?"

"I'm worried."

"Ah," Jessy murmured, leaning back again and smiling. It was strange. So very strange. She hadn't seen him in forever, they'd been so much younger.

But now she felt as if . . .

They really had known one another forever. As if years hadn't gone by. As if they were as close as friends could possibly be, as if . . .

As if there was something special between them. Chemistry. More.

Except that . . .

As close as she felt to him, as attracted as she was to him, there was something . . .

Something he wasn't telling her.

They reached the Danson ranch. He drew up on the driveway before the front door. She reached for the door handle, and he turned the car off.

She laughed softly. "Wyatt, we're here—in front of the door!"

He nodded. "Sorry, you know my mother! She taught me you always see a lady right to her door."

"My door is right there."

"And I'm walking you to it." He laughed. "Hey, come on!"

"Okay, okay, but it's broad daylight; the hands are all about, I'm sure. People start early at a horse ranch, you know. And I'm sure Samantha is up and about."

He exited the car and walked around to her door, opening it for her. And he walked up the porch steps with her and waited for her to open the door.

He didn't leave.

"Wyatt—"

"Step in. I want to see if Samantha is up and about."

She was.

Samantha came rushing out of the kitchen, smooshing Jessy in a warm hug, pulling away and looking at Wyatt.

"Thank you so much for calling and letting us know what had happened. Of course, now the press has gotten hold of it all and . . . oh, Jessy! It's amazing. You two saved that young lady! A reporter was at the hospital.

They don't have your names; I was going to call in and tell them who found her—"

"No, no, please!" Wyatt said. He glanced at Jessy.

"He's right. Please, we gave law enforcement all that they needed. We don't want our names associated. Oh! And I talked with my folks. They're going to be able to make it out here for Christmas, and I don't want to worry them. I mean . . ."

She paused, glancing at Wyatt again.

"We're going to need to warn them, just like everyone out here needs to be warned that people are out there, that they've now sent a woman to a hospital and nearly killed a girl. But Jessy is right. I think it will be a lot better if we keep any involvement that we had quiet."

"Of course, of course . . . but our household knows!" she said. "And Wyatt McFarlane, if you think you're not going to tell your parents about this . . ."

"Sam, I will tell my parents, I promise," Wyatt told her.

Sam nodded, but she was frowning. "What the two of you did was heroic! Why wouldn't you want people to know?"

"There are a few reasons," Wyatt said.

"And they are?" Samantha asked him.

"Those people are still out there. I wouldn't want them determining we might know more than we do. They're dangerous, Sam. Let's not give them any reason to come after the two of us."

"Okay, okay, I do understand that could be a concern, I guess," Samantha said. Her eyes widened. "Oh! Did she know anything, did that poor girl see anything, does she know who—".

"No. She didn't know anything at all. They came up behind her. She heard her mother fall, she rushed to the kitchen to see what had happened . . . and they threw a feed bag, probably burlap, over her head. She was overpowered and blinded. They dumped her in an old hole off the property of the house. People searched everywhere—but beneath the ground. Still, Samantha, please . . ."

"I will make sure Cody knows that we are not to say anything at all. Though, if those wretches were to come here, well, we'd give them what-for! Between Cody and the hands—and I bet I can be pretty lethal with a rolling pin—we'd give them bloody hell!"

Jessy glanced at Wyatt, smiling, and saw that he was smiling, too.

Samantha could be tough with all her skinny energy and determination!

"Mom and Dad will be here soon—" Jessy began.

"Oh! That's so wonderful. But we don't have a tree up yet or anything—"

"How about this," Wyatt offered. "I'll pick Jessy up around four in the afternoon—we both really need some sleep—and we'll head out and get a tree. You can get Andrews up in the attic during the day to bring down the boxes of ornaments, and we'll get Christmas all set up here by tomorrow night."

"Okay, Wyatt, except, between all of us—"

"No, really!" Wyatt said, smiling at Jessy. "I'd like to take Jessy to get a tree, and I'd love to be here to help set up. Our place is all done—you know my mom. It's been done since the day after Thanksgiving. So, Jessy, if it's okay with you, I'd be honored to go and pick up a tree with you and help get it set up!"

"I, um, sure, of course," Jessy said.

She wasn't sure why he was so determined to see her again.

And she thought she was a fool to be so happy that he did.

This wasn't home. She'd be leaving. And she sincerely doubted the man planned on following her to New York.

"I'll pick you up!" he told her.

"I will be ready by four!" she promised.

Finally, Wyatt left, warning Samantha that even if Cody and the hands were up and about, they needed to keep the door locked.

Jessy impulsively hugged Samantha and told her, "I've really, truly got to get some sleep!"

"Of course! You get on up there. I'll just check on you around three-thirty and see that you're awake," Samantha assured her.

"Perfect. And good night. Or good day—or whatever it is now!" Jessy said.

She ran up the stairs, ready to crash into bed. She didn't disrobe, she just kicked off her shoes.

She'd had a shower last evening.

Another shower would wait until she'd had some sleep.

But lying there, as exhausted as she was, she didn't sleep immediately.

There was something about Wyatt . . .

Yes, she felt an incredibly great attraction for him. She'd had a crush on him as a kid. But she was just seeing him again.

And as intense as the night had been . . .

It was frightening.

Frightening to know just how much she wanted to be with him because it was crazy, so very crazy. There was also, she felt, something that he wasn't telling her.

And not even that seemed to matter.

Then, somewhere in her thoughts, she did close her eyes.

And sleep.

And still . . .

Somehow, the man managed to haunt her dreams.

CHAPTER 4

Wyatt was never quite sure when he learned that he could go a good forty-eight hours without sleep.

Maybe he trained himself to do it when he was in college, when too many interests tore him in different directions.

After he left Jessy at her home, he headed back to the offices in Colorado Springs; he knew that his Supervisory Special Agent would be waiting for him.

And he was. Seeing Wyatt arrive, SSA Anthony Vargas motioned to him to join him in his office.

"First, thank you, and congratulations. This is still a mess, but it's my understanding that poor girl wouldn't have made it much longer. You saved a life, but what I want to know is this—how the hell did you know to go out there looking for her? We tore that property apart; we went to every neighboring house and property— how the hell did you know where to look? Wyatt, I know you don't want to believe that a friend could be involved, but were you given a hint, did someone say something?"

Vargas had spent almost thirty years in the bureau;

he was Colorado born and bred but had served across
the country. Now, he was a focused and serious man, bald
as a buzzard, but lean, fit, and professional, as befitted
his position.

"Sir, I swear to you that friendship wouldn't influence me when we're searching for someone who is not
just robbing people, but threatening their lives," Wyatt
told him. "But this had nothing to do with anyone who
was even in the area when the robbery took place.
Kelly Danson, my family's closest neighbor, passed
away recently. His granddaughter, Jessy Danson, was a
friend of mine—or, at the least a close acquaintance
when we were growing up since our families were
always friendly. She arrived just yesterday from New
York. I invited her to the club last night, and when she
heard about what happened, she started telling me about
outbuildings on her property that had been forgotten
because new facilities for various purposes had been
built. She insisted we go out there. I knew I heard a cry.
I could not find a building—derelict or otherwise—and
the only other possibility was a bunker or storage area
underground."

"This woman who helped you has only been here
about a day now?" Vargas asked.

"That's right."

"You don't think she's been in touch with someone
here—"

"Sir, I know that she has not."

Vargas let out a sigh, shaking his head. "And you
don't think any of your other friends or acquaintances

have figured out that you're undercover as yourself with the bureau?"

Wyatt shook his head.

It had been a strange journey for him. Music, yes, he'd always loved music. And he'd also loved the ranch and the great state of Colorado, the beauty of the mountains and plains. He'd grown up at rodeos, bull riding and barrel racing.

But he'd been a freshman in college when Gayle Meyers had been kidnapped. And it had been the work of an undercover agent that had led to her discovery.

It had been a lot like this situation . . .

Gayle Meyers had been found in an abandoned warehouse, unconscious, barely responsive—but she was alive today because of the dedication and work of one woman, a trained agent who had inveigled her way into the group that had been committing a series of crimes, one of which had been witnessed by Gayle Meyers.

Music had become, ironically, *second fiddle,* in his quest to discover just exactly what he wanted to do with his future.

Classes in crime scene investigation, the law, and the role of law enforcement had begun to fill his schedule.

And he'd known, and the academy had been his first step right out of college.

He was great at undercover work, which meant he did travel constantly for business, and he'd been at it for years. His home office was there, Vargas was his immediate superior, but the travel to work in other areas was good. It kept him from places where he was a known quantity.

But then this strange situation had arisen and profilers—and law enforcement officers and agents who weren't profilers—all believed that someone local had to be involved.

And the belief was that houses and ranches were watched. Usually, the criminals waited until they knew no one would be around.

But then they had grown bolder.

And thus, they'd put a woman in the intensive care unit of a hospital and nearly killed a teenaged girl.

"Well, you should probably get some sleep. And I'm going to assume that you're not being influenced—"

"Sir, no. I'll admit, I'm pretty close to the men who are in the band I play with, but I've also been able to spend time with them. I know where they've been, and what they've been doing. I have had my suspicions regarding one of the hands at the Danson ranch."

"And you have solid ground?"

"If I had solid ground, I would have told you, and an arrest would have been made by now. And I assure you, my emotions regarding anyone would be outweighed a thousand times over by the fact that a teenaged girl could have died after that last heist, not to mention the girl's mother, who was still in the intensive care unit last night."

"What is your suspicion?" Vargas asked him.

Wyatt hesitated; he hadn't meant to. He was serious; whatever exactly was going on and between whoever, it was getting worse.

"There's a hand at the Danson ranch I'm keeping an eye on," Wyatt told Vargas. "David Benson. He's a fellow of about five-eleven or maybe six feet even, but he's built like a bull—lots of power to force someone around with or without a gun. I've known Cody Connelly—their ranch manager—since I was a kid. He's a good boss. But a few days ago, I stopped over there. There's that rodeo coming up the Saturday before Christmas, and when I'm in town, I always showcase one of their quarter horses in the barrel racing."

"And you win a lot, I take it," Vargas offered dryly.

Wyatt shrugged. "I think I rode a horse before I could walk, sir. My family has a dairy cattle ranch, but riding has always been part of handling the herd. Anyway, when I was over there, I had gone to see Cody about what horse he wanted me to work this year. When I was leaving, I stopped and chatted with the housekeeper, and I could hear Cody talking to David and he was angry. It was the day after one of the robberies, and Cody was angry with David for being late or for not showing up at all. I wasn't sure which. But while they aren't required to live at the ranch, the hands all have housing in a dormitory-style building that's located behind the stables. David has a place there, and whether he was or wasn't there that morning, I don't know. I mean, the man just may have been out late with friends—"

"And those friends might have been criminals," Vargas said.

Wyatt shrugged. "Where I question myself is in this—whoever is doing this knows what the hell they're doing. Forensic teams haven't been able to find a single fingerprint that didn't belong or so much as an epithelial cell. David Benson doesn't have a criminal record—he's accrued parking tickets, but nothing more. I think he'd be great brawn when needed, but I don't know how or where he might have learned to be so careful. At the Dunworth house, Chrissie was taken by surprise, a feed bag was quickly thrown over her head, and she saw nothing. Her mother was clocked from behind with a figurine that was easily available where she had been standing. Nothing on it—except for her blood and tissue. Someone knows—"

"You can learn just about anything on YouTube these days," Vargas said wearily.

"Still, I think we're looking for someone who may have been in prison at some time in his life, someone who might have learned from his—or her—mistakes."

"But among your acquaintances—"

"No such person. But that doesn't mean that I don't know someone who might know someone. And of course, I could be entirely wrong."

"But then again," Vargas said, "after everything we've done, we've still got nothing. Nothing at all. No one has even noticed a car that shouldn't have been somewhere or seen the same kind of car. And after all this, we don't have a damned lead. So, do it, Wyatt. Go with your gut. See if you can get anywhere. This is getting worse and worse. The only thing is, the damned situation won't turn into a cold case—because these perps show no signs of stopping!"

Wyatt nodded.

"Get out of here. Before someone sees you."

He nodded. Time to head back to his own place, grab a few hours of sleep, and get back over to Jessy's place.

He winced. He realized that he didn't want to go home.

He wanted to go straight over to the Danson ranch.

Because Jessy was there now. And he sure as hell didn't want her hurt!

He grimaced. It was a horrible position to be in. Because seeing Jessy again, being with her, getting to know the adult version of the beautiful child he'd loved to torment . . .

It didn't matter. It didn't matter who she was. He'd protect a victim with his own life no matter what, but . . .

He had to also remember that whatever he discovered, his actions had to be within the law.

But . . .

There was something more. He hadn't wanted their names out on anything that had to do with the discovery of Chrissie Dunworth in the old bunker in the field.

He wasn't worried about himself. Dealing with criminals was what he did.

But he was deeply concerned when it came to Jessy. He'd told himself the ranch was a crowded house— even if David Benson was guilty of something, he was surrounded by Cody, Samantha, Tate, and Eddie.

He wouldn't pull anything off at the Danson ranch. He wouldn't try. While the ranch hands didn't walk around armed all the time, they all had guns, which was legal in Colorado.

And they knew how to use them. Something that came about when you lived with horses, cows, and other creatures far from the busy streets of a town where police might be frequently cruising around.

Out here, carrying a gun might equal survival. Not that bad things occurred often. The point was that they could occur.

So . . .

Jessy would most probably only be in any danger if she went off the property. He had to make sure she wasn't off the property—unless she was with him. And of course, her parents would be coming in.

But how much could they protect her? Her mother was a teacher. Her father was a brilliant tech fellow who had now lived in a major city for years and years.

No, they could be victimized as easily as Chrissie and her mom had been.

Jessy was safe, he told himself, as long as she was at the ranch.

Unless, of course, they were all in on it?

He gave himself a mental shake. Unlikely. Oh, so unlikely!

But still . . .

What if?

Jessy was glad she'd never made a set time to meet with Jenson Applegate.

She was surprised that she managed to drag herself up after about four and a half hours of sleep.

She could shower and dress in a flash; she did so, then hurried downstairs to discover that Cody, Samantha, and Jenson were all there. And when she appeared on the stairs, they burst into applause.

She stared at them, stunned.

"We all heard what you did!" Jenson told her. "Jessy! Do you realize what you did? You saved a life! There was a press conference earlier. Don't worry—they didn't give your names out, but they said the actions of a few citizens saved that poor girl's life! Oh, Jessy, your grandfather would be so proud of you! You were so heroic!"

"Well, thank you," Jessy said. "But I wasn't heroic at all. I just started thinking about outbuildings, and I was really wrong. She was in a bunker beneath the ground. We got lucky—"

"But there would have been no getting lucky if you hadn't thought to go out there!" Cody said. "Seriously, Jessy, you are . . . well . . ."

He broke off, looking at Jenson.

"I think that I know what we're up to here, Jessy. And I know you're doing the best that you can for everyone. But you want to leave. You want to live in New York—"

"I'll come back!" she promised. "There hasn't been a year in my life when I haven't been out here a few times—"

"Because your grandfather was alive," Samantha said.

Jessy hesitated, then told Jenson, "I didn't get a chance to tell you this yet. I talked to my folks yesterday. They're due out here the day after tomorrow."

Jenson frowned. "You—you'd like to wait on your father for our business meeting?" he asked.

"Yeah, I would. Nothing here is going to change!" she assured him. "Sam has always managed the house. Cody, you keep everything going great with the horses, with our breeding program, with sales! I know you even check out the people who come to buy one of our horses; you make sure that our animals are going to good homes. Nothing will change!"

Jenson looked at her and nodded slowly.

He smiled. "Tomorrow, then. Hey, Samantha just put out a great-looking sandwich board. Thought I was going to be skipping lunch. I'm on my way into the dining room."

"Me, too," Cody said.

"Well, then! I will join you all!" Jessy said with a smile.

Wyatt wasn't due at the house until four, and since she'd slept through the concept of breakfast, and it might be quite a while until dinner, lunch sounded good.

But she hadn't made it all the way to the dining room when there was a tap at the door.

"Got it!" Samantha said, hurrying over to look through the peephole, smile, and open the door.

Wyatt had come early.

"Sorry!" he said to Jessy as he stepped in. "I'm early. I was awake so—"

"Wait! He gets applause, too!" Jenson proclaimed, and they all broke into applause.

"It was all Jessy!" Wyatt said with a shrug, grinning

at her. "Oh, and it's information we're not putting out there!"

"Got it!" Cody said. "We don't want any of those sickies to come after our Jessy!"

"It's just best to keep it all in-house," Wyatt said.

"We were about to have lunch," Jessy said. "Want to join us?"

"Wow—great! Now I'm delighted I came early," he said. "Sam, I'm not going to be putting anyone out—"

"Oh, come on, Wyatt McFarlane!" Samantha said. "How long have you known me? Of course there's plenty, and you're always welcome to join us!"

They all wandered into the dining room. David Benson and Eddie Andrews were already in the larger dining room, where Samantha had set out bread, crackers, cheeses, meats, and a bowl filled with fresh fruits. They looked up when they were joined by the others, and David was quick to greet them, saying, "Wow! Look, Eddie, we're being joined by our new boss and local heroine—and the hero next door! Yeah, guys!"

"Well, thanks!" Wyatt answered. "So, everyone here knows. But—"

"Oh! We know not to say anything to anyone else," Eddie assured him.

"Thanks, good," Wyatt said.

"Well, I guess our gang is all here—except for Tate," Jessy said.

"One of us always spells the others," Cody told her. "Even at night; I thought you knew that. Tate is out with the horses; he'll come in as soon as one of us heads out."

"I guess I forgot," Jessy said. She smiled. They didn't have a dog as big and fierce looking as Wyatt's Bandit, but they had two German shepherds on the property, and they were quick to give warning that someone had come. "I guess that I always think of Misty and Morgan as being on the job."

"And they are the best!" Cody assured her. "We've just always liked to keep on the alert, you know. It wasn't that big a deal, but about six years ago, someone slipped in at night and hit the Holliston ranch down the road a couple of miles. Opened the gates in the night and stole a few of the old man's prized bulls. Anyway . . . we listen for Misty and Morgan, and just keep an eye open. It's not that hard. We shift the schedule around, because we do kind of have social lives."

Eddie laughed. "'Kind of'—that explains it! But hey, the rodeo is coming up, Jessy. That's something you do need to decide. You going to ride this year?"

"Wow. Um, just give me tonight to think on that, okay? I won't have a chance to get out there anyway, today. My dad has been cleared to travel. He and my mom are coming. Wyatt and I are going to go and pick out a tree at the tree farm, come back, and oh! If one of you can get up into the attic and bring down the decorations, that would be great!"

"Will do!" Eddie assured her.

"And you're all standing around staring at one another. Eat!" Samantha ordered.

Grins followed her words, and they began passing

around the plates that held all the different goodies that Samantha had put out for them.

Cheese, lettuce, and tomatoes worked just fine for Jessy. She saw that at her side, Wyatt grinned.

And he created a similar sandwich, opting for an apple when she picked out an orange.

The talk around the table was casual at first. David was extolling an action film he'd seen in Colorado Springs the previous weekend, and Cody was talking about the fact how he was grateful that these days, everything came to TV eventually and he could just kick back and watch.

"That's 'cause you're an old man!" David told Cody.

"You're not that much younger!" Cody reminded David.

"I think you hit the big five-oh last year—oh, wait, that was three years ago, and I'm just a handsome and charming forty-six!" David said, laughing. "Still hopeful that romance is out there somewhere. And I'm not going to find it here with you sorry dudes!"

"Ah, but wait!" Cody argued. "We had a pretty young thing out here just last week with her pretty, older cousin!"

"I don't think she really wanted to buy a horse," David said. "I think she met our boy toy, Mr. Eddie Andrews, there, at Murphy's Pub one night and wanted to see if she could . . . well, you know! See the boy again."

Eddie groaned. "Her father is Ned Tyson, winner of many a rodeo championship. She did want to see our horses."

"Well, there, see, it still doesn't hurt having a young buck on the property who can keep us all . . . busy!" Cody said.

"Ah, you like Murphy's, huh?" Wyatt said to Eddie. "We didn't see you there last night."

"Yeah, sorry, I knew you were playing. But the old coot over there had me on night duty!" Eddie said. "Next time. But hey! You got out there, right? That's where you two were before you headed out . . . to save that girl!"

"We were at the pub, yeah; and it's still a great place to go," Jessy said.

"Next time you have a gig," Eddie said, holding up a piece of bread as if he could keep Cody from hearing his teasing words, "I'll have you speak to the old coot here and get him to make sure I'm not on night duty!"

Cody groaned, and they all laughed.

Soon enough, they'd finished lunch and Wyatt looked at Jessy. "Ready?"

"Onward to purchase a tree," she said, adding, "Wyatt, honestly, I mean, I could do this by myself—"

"And it's more fun if we do it together. The tree farm offers this super little place, too, where they have great hot chocolate. Naturally, it's good business sense. People come from all around to head out there. You pick out your tree—and sip hot chocolate while the employees get it strapped onto your car. They do it all day for days on end, so they're really good at it. But I brought one of the trucks today, so we don't even need to worry about a stranger scratching up a good vehicle or a rented car," he told her.

"Okay! Tree time, and thank you!" Jessy told him. "Sam, guys—"

"Happy hunting!" Cody said. "And I'll head on out with you so that Tate can come on in and get his food."

They walked out together. Misty and Morgan had been running around the front pasture, but seeing Wyatt, Cody, and Jessy emerge from the house, they came leaping through the slats in the fence to greet them.

Jessy was always amazed that the dogs remembered her. They were comparatively young, from the same litter, about six years old now.

There had always been dogs—shepherds usually—at the ranch. Her grandfather had adored dogs and thought there was nothing quite as good as a dog for protection—despite Cody having someone on guard duty all the time.

She gave the dogs loving pets. Cody warned them to behave, and Wyatt gave them attention as well.

Then she and Wyatt waved to Cody and headed out to Wyatt's truck.

"You must not have slept long," Jessy told him as he revved the truck into gear.

He shrugged. "I've never been able to sleep during the day."

"Even when you're up all night?"

He shrugged, looking at her. "Well, you were up and about when I got here."

"Yeah, you're right. I'm not much on sleeping during the day, either. So, this tree farm is not far?"

"Five miles. We'll be there in no time. Even if we are on country roads. Oh, wow, hmm. Country road!

I'll play some John Denver. Of course, the country road he's singing about is West Virginia, but . . ."

She laughed. "John Denver. One of my dad's favorites. Go for it!"

"Great! Compare me to your dad."

"Hey, I love my dad. And tons of old music!" she assured him. She glanced over at him. He was smiling, but she sensed something behind his smile.

Just as she sensed several times that . . .

That there was something she didn't know. Something he wasn't telling her.

"What?" he asked.

"You're suspicious."

"I'm suspicious?"

"Yeah, I keep thinking there's something I should know, but I don't."

He laughed. "Hey, I'm not married. I swear. If and when I do get married, I won't be following other women around."

"Aha! So, you are following me around!"

He groaned. "Jessy—"

"Now, come on, my friend. Tall, dark, and handsome. Cool as ever with his guitar! You mean to tell me you're not seeing anyone?"

He laughed. "I'm not going to tell you that I've never seen anyone, but no, I'm not seeing anyone now." He shrugged. "Business. I've had to travel a lot lately. I also work with a studio in Colorado Springs—"

"How does that make you travel?"

"Oh, well, not that. But we have all kinds of contracts

with companies who purchase our milk, cheese, and other products. I wind up being on the road a lot."

"But you're here—mostly. Or at your condo in the Keys?"

"I wish I could be at the condo way more than I am."

"Yeah, but that's cool, since you're going to be lending it to me!"

He groaned. "It would be fun if we could be there at the same time. Oh, but wait! I just realized that I should be asking the same questions. There isn't a Mr. Jessy anywhere?"

She laughed softly. "Not married. And same answer. I've seen people, of course. But . . . no one ever seriously. I work alone most of the time. And the author I work with most often—the children's author on that book you say you bought—"

"I did buy it."

"Well, thanks. Anyway, the author is a friend of mine. We get out now and then, but we're just friends and have never been more. I know his wife, and she's a doll. Oh, yeah, I get to gallery openings—"

"Speaking of which, there's a gallery opening in Colorado Springs next week. You should get something in it!"

"Wyatt, if the opening is next week, the show is already planned," she told him. "And I will definitely get in to see it! But the rodeo is Saturday, and Christmas will be Tuesday right after, so . . ."

"The rodeo is Saturday; we can go to the opening on Sunday. It's a weekend deal."

"You don't need to go to a gallery opening just because of me."

He looked her way, smiling. "But I'd love to go to a gallery opening with you. You could keep me from making any stupid comments."

She laughed. "Somehow, I have the feeling that you can go just about anywhere and fit right in—and not make stupid comments."

"Can't count on that!" he told her. And then he glanced her way.

And there was something in his eyes, in his look . . .

That seemed honest.

"I'd love to go anywhere with you," he said softly.

And he meant it, she realized.

It was too insane! She hadn't seen him for years. Yes, he'd been a childhood crush, but just that. And now, they had barely even touched, and she loved every minute spent in his company and wanted more, and it seemed as if . . .

As if she had slipped back into something that was perfect and natural, and yet it was a place where, in truth, she had never been before.

Coming home. But she wasn't home, New York was home, and yet . . .

Home would never really be a where.

She gave herself a mental shake. She had discovered that the teen who had teased her had grown into an incredible man. And it was nice to be with him, and they'd had some intense moments in a very short period of time.

And there was nothing wrong with enjoying her time with him while she was here!

"Well, a tree! The objective for now!"

"And we're almost there," he said.

She could see the property ahead of them, a huge field covered with Christmas trees of various sizes. As they drove closer, she saw the driveway that led to parking—and a rectangular building that apparently offered a fireplace and more within.

"Tree first," Wyatt said, exiting the truck.

Jessy quickly slid out herself, walking around to join him. He pointed to the path that led into the grove of trees.

She smiled; it was easy to see that she was late in the season—many people, she knew, liked to decorate for Christmas when Thanksgiving was barely over. Of course, most people did decorate before now.

"Big tree, medium tree? I mean, it's your tree, but I'm going to suggest a fairly large tree, not a little one, because if it's a little tree, it might disappear in the size of the ranch house. I can see where it would go—your call, of course—but there's a great spot by that old Duncan Phyfe sofa in the parlor against the wall, far enough from the fireplace and easy enough to stack with presents. Hmm. I just realized that I haven't been Christmas shopping. Ouch. Well, thankfully, there are places that deliver overnight!"

Jessy groaned. "Christmas, and I didn't even think about . . . I'm horrible! I guess that I was finishing up on a deadline, my grandfather was failing, and I was spending time with him. Then he died, and . . . I mean, he was old and he was happy and he felt that he'd been gifted with a beautiful life. I got to hold his hand, and he was peaceful, and I guess . . ."

"No matter how beautiful his life, how peaceful his death, you loved him, and you missed him. And then you came out here just a few weeks later; that's a lot!" Wyatt said.

"Well, it's been almost a month," Jessy murmured. "He was with us on Thanksgiving, and the . . . It was almost as if he waited for that last Thanksgiving! Anyway, as his granddaughter, I need to make sure that the staff gets their presents—"

"The ranch made money—it's always made money," Wyatt assured her. "I can suggest you just give the staff money—that's always appreciated!"

"Yeah, but my mom and dad are coming . . . and I do have friends back in New York!"

"And when you're back in New York, you can take care of that. Look, there—it's perfect. Well, I think it's perfect. Not huge, but nice and full. So what do you think?"

"It's—perfect."

"Ah, good. Great minds think alike, eh?" he teased. *Maybe too much.*

"It's, um, a tree!" she said. "Anyway, let's go with it! I'm ready for my hot chocolate now!"

One of the men working the farm hurried over to them, and Wyatt pointed out the tree. He was given a coupon to pay for it, and Wyatt described his truck.

The tree would be delivered to the vehicle.

They turned and headed back to the building. There was one free table, and Wyatt suggested she take it while he dealt with the tree.

"But it's my tree. I need to pay—"

"Like you said, it's a tree! I've got it. Just order me a large hot chocolate—oh, they'll put a shot of espresso in it. That might be good now. And they make amazing Christmas shortbread. We could be like kids again with hot chocolate and cookies!"

He steered her toward the table and left her.

The place was nice. A fire was burning, and the mantel was handsomely decorated with strands of ivy and flowers. People sat about chatting in the warmth of the room, and for a minute, it was nice to just sit back.

When he headed back to the table, Wyatt had a strange look on his face. He was grinning.

He took the chair next to hers, leaned over, and planted a quick kiss on her lips.

She was startled, to say the least.

Not offended or angry, just . . .

"Sorry!" he said lightly. "You sat right under the mistletoe!"

She started to laugh. And without thinking, she leaned over the table and kissed him back.

Her kiss just a little slower and longer, a little wetter . . .

It was, after all, a public place.

But when she pulled away . . .

She knew.

The intimate touches they had shared were something they had both wanted, even if they both wondered how and why.

A prelude, perhaps, to . . .

Much, much more.

CHAPTER 5

Wyatt was pleased to discover that the Danson household staff had been working in their absence.

The Christmas tree stand was ready for the tree and several boxes filled with ornaments and decorations awaited them in the parlor.

"Hey!"

It was Eddie, cheerful and energetic, who first welcomed them back to the house—he was putting down one of the boxes marked "Christmas" in large lettering.

"Hey, yourself. And thank you!" Jessy said.

"Well, I hope this helps because Cody just got a message from the rodeo folks—we have to have our paperwork filled out by first thing in the morning. And, as you know, we'd all really love it if you'd enter the barrel racing competitions," Eddie said. "I can get all this set up—not decorate, I promise—just get the tree in the stand and open all the boxes and that way—"

Jessy smiled. "Yeah, I guess I should go and see our guys and gals out in the stables—I didn't see them out in the paddocks. They're all in the stables?"

"Yep. We were thinking that you rode Shiloh last year—"

"And I will go and talk to Shiloh again," she promised. "And Eddie, seriously, thank you all. My grandfather would have been prepared a month ago and—"

"We lost him and that had to be so hard on you—it was hard on all of us," Eddie said. "But knowing that you would be here, well, that helped!"

Wyatt saw that Eddie was sincere and Jessy was touched by his words.

But, of course, by the nature of his work, he thought about all he knew regarding Eddie Andrews.

Just turned thirty, he'd been an excellent student in school—but he hadn't pursued education beyond a stint in junior college. That might have been financial. His parents had been killed in an automobile accident when he'd been seventeen; he'd lived with an aunt, now deceased as well, until he was eighteen.

He'd met Kelly Danson at a rodeo while still in junior college and had come to the ranch while finishing out his last year. He was, if sources were current on this, casually seeing a young woman named Cathy Barrow who was a salesgirl at a boutique in Colorado Springs.

Nothing suspicious there, except, of course, in his mind, Wyatt could make up just about any scenario.

Then again, he trusted animals and their instincts more than he tended to trust people—and the horses and the dogs seemed to love him.

"Are you going to ride at the rodeo?" Jessy asked Eddie.

He winced. "I don't mind a stint in the bull riding—

I can fall off an animal really, really well! But I would so prefer you doing the barrel racing!"

"Okay, then. Thanks, Eddie. I'll go out and . . . have a discussion with Shiloh!"

Jessy looked at Wyatt and Wyatt gave her a smile and a grin.

They headed on out to the stables. Tate was on the front porch as they exited the house—where he had been when they arrived. But it was six in the evening and at this time of the year, chilly and almost dark already.

"Hey again!" Tate said.

"On watch duty, eh?" Wyatt asked.

"You know it," Tate said. He shrugged. "Cody just wants a human being helping out our critters. No big deal. I sit out here and play with my phone or read or . . . whatever! And everyone gets their turn on our night duty shifts, so . . . of course, sorry! Jessy, you're here now and all the calls will be yours!"

"Oh, hell, no!" Jessy told him, grinning. "You guys have kept this place going great for years and years and I wouldn't touch what you're doing right with a ten-foot pole! Anyway, we're heading to the stables. I haven't . . . pretty terrible, but I haven't actually said hello to the horses yet, and this is a horse ranch, so . . ."

Tate brightened up. "You're going to ride!"

"Yeah, I guess so. But I'll have to start working like crazy tomorrow!" Jessy said.

Tate grinned. "It's like riding a bike, you know, just that it's a horse instead. It hasn't been that long, Jessy! You were out here last year, and you did great!"

"Well, thanks," Jessy told him.

She smiled and started down the steps. Wyatt grimaced at Tate and followed her.

And, of course, started thinking about Tate Laughton.

The man had turned forty-nine last April and Wyatt had been around for his birthday party along with just about every ranch hand and owner in the area. They'd spilled out of Murphy's Pub, where the party had been held.

Naturally, the teasing had been about it being his last birthday before the big five-oh, when, of course, he'd have to remember that he'd been around for half a century.

Tate had taken it all in good humor.

He'd been married once in his twenties but was long divorced from his wife. He was known to keep company now and then with a woman in town, a widow named Clare Mortimer, who was, in fact, one of the artists who would be featured at the gallery opening coming up. Wyatt had met her a few times; she was attractive, forty-five, and, like Tate, barely graying despite the natural ravages of time. She was nice, cheerful, and, like Tate, energetic. She once told Wyatt that anyone could stay young—at least mentally. Of course, what time might do to the bones had to be handled by doing all the right things.

Tate was born in New Mexico and had worked on a horse ranch there before coming to the Danson ranch almost thirty years ago.

A good suspect for a robber? Probably not.

But then . . .

Was David Benson actually a good suspect?

Wyatt was back to thinking about the friendships he and his parents had enjoyed through the years, but one thing he had learned during his tenure with the bureau was that you never really, *really,* knew another person or what went on in their hearts and minds.

Then again, because of his own heart and mind, it might be good that he was concentrating on the personalities at the ranch.

Though, of course, David Benson might be guilty of nothing more than a night out on the town. But there was also that strange thing that went along with his studies and his years in law enforcement, something not really a part of either . . .

His *sixth sense* telling him that something was very, very wrong.

"So . . ." Jessy murmured as they headed for the stables. She smiled at Wyatt. "My grandfather was my teacher. He said that the key aspect was remembering to maintain the proper balance and position on the horse. And I'm hoping—"

"You're hoping; I'm betting on you. Come on, riding a bike, riding a horse . . . Jessy, you'll be fine. And it will mean so very much to everyone here," he assured her.

"Okay!"

The night lights were on in the stables as they always were; it was dim enough to allow the horses to sleep, but there was enough light so that they weren't stumbling in the dark.

Misty and Morgan were on duty in the center of the

stables, hopping up with little woofs to greet them, tails wagging away.

And, naturally, they took a few minutes with the dogs.

"You have a pet in New York?" Wyatt asked Jessy.

She laughed softly. "A cat. Clover. He's old now, a rescue, but a sweetie. He's with a friend of mine now—I mean, the good thing about a cat is that it can be very self-sufficient. But I had no idea how long I'd be gone, so he's with Sally Granger, one of my neighbors, who has two cats of her own. And, bizarrely enough, all the cats get along."

"Nice. I guess you didn't think about bringing Clover out here."

"Well, I wasn't going to subject him to the flight when . . ."

"When you're not staying. Got it. But hey, it's great that you're going to be here—while you're here. Down, Misty, Morgan! We've got to check in on the horses."

It was almost as if the dogs understood Wyatt. They fell into step as they walked along the stable area.

Rocker was sound asleep, on the ground and not standing. Juniper was asleep standing. Philly Girl walked over for some strokes on the nose. Blueridge also wanted some attention as did Haydon and Braxton.

They all had long professional names on their papers, but in the stable, they were just part of the family.

Finally, they reached Shiloh's stall.

The running quarter horse stood a good seventeen hands tall; he was a handsome buckskin with an amazing personality. The animal snorted and nosed Jessy as if she was a long-lost relative.

In a way, she was.

And Jessy reacted to the horse. Her smile, the way she talked to the animal and stroked his nose . . .

She might not want to stay in Colorado, but . . .

"Don't go getting too attached!" he warned her. "Shiloh really will not fit in a New York City apartment."

"Haha, funny, funny!" Jessy returned. But she smiled at him. "Tomorrow, I'm going to need to start working with him. Of course, that one paddock has always been outfitted with barrels so that the abilities of our young horses can be shown when they're up for sale. All I'll need to do is wake up and start practicing, but, oh! I still haven't heard from my mom about when to pick her and Dad up at the airport!"

"Why don't you call her?" Wyatt suggested.

"Right. I'll do that. It's not that late yet . . . She and Dad have a tendency to be in bed by ten, but . . ."

She pulled out her phone and hit a speed dial number. She smiled at him as her mom answered, and then she began to tell her mother that something was all right.

A minute later she ended the call and looked at him.

"Well, I can work tomorrow. They couldn't get a flight and don't get here until Friday night."

"Then I'll come out and work with you."

"But you're not going to barrel ride?"

"No, chicken. I'm not going to compete against you," he told her.

"Oh, yeah! I'm sure I really scare you," she said lightly. "But . . . it sounds like you work a lot. I mean, you don't need to mess up your own life to be with me."

"I told you. I love being anywhere with you," he said.

She smiled. And then they were just looking at one another, and the horse hair, dog hair, and the fact that they were in the stables meant nothing at all. They were close already, together at the door to Shiloh's stall.

And it seemed nothing at all that they both made the slightest move, and she was in his arms, and the kiss they had instigated with mistletoe over their heads suddenly became something instigated as one, long and deep, bodies together, arms around one another . . .

Then, almost as one as well, they eased apart, grinning, with Jessy saying, "We are kind of in the middle of—"

"The stables. And people will come outside and in here soon enough if we don't make an appearance back in the house," he agreed.

"Christmas setup!" she told him.

"Right. And let's get to it!"

"And lots of nosy people hanging around."

Misty woofed as if in agreement.

"And I don't really care. But I shall be happy to be extremely discreet!"

"But . . ."

"But?"

"To be continued?" she asked softly.

Something ripped through him. Lightning. Desire, of course. But again, he was thinking that it was so incredibly strange, so many years had passed, their lives had gone in different directions, and yet in similar ways. Diving, and NYC or not, she still loved her horses—and dogs, as well as her cat!

And tomorrow . . .

His chance.

To study and talk with David Benson, press his suspicions . . .

And be with Jessy. And yet, what would she feel if she knew what he really did for work?

He winced inwardly. Because everything about this was true.

"Tree!" Jessy said, heading out of the stables.

He followed.

Tate greeted them on the porch. They chatted for just a minute and walked on in.

Then, the rest of the household was inside. Samantha, of course, Cody, David, and even Jenson Applegate.

"So, we waited for instructions from the big boss!" Cody said, sweeping out an arm to indicate the boxes.

"Ah, guys, come on!" Jessy begged.

"But you are an artist," David reminded her.

She laughed. "On paper or with paper or whatever! Anyway . . . let's do it up the way my grandfather liked. Mantel with the runner and the little angels, colorful globe ornaments dispersed with the special ones he collected, Disney and others. And we can put the larger things—like the Santa Claus with the kids—on the coffee table."

"Okay. I'm on ornaments," Eddie said. "Cody—"

"With you. I'll get them, you place them," Cody said.

"I'll get some of the big guys out," David offered.

"Okay, I'll be second fiddle on that enterprise," Jenson told them.

"Mantel," Jessy said.

"I'll help you on that," Wyatt told her.

"And I'll go get some coffee, tea, and cocoa going!" Samantha said. "Oh! Jessy, you and Wyatt missed dinner! I'll put out some little sandwiches with Christmas cookies!"

"Hey, and it's a Christmas setup!" Jenson said. "I think there should be a nice choice on whether those drinks are spiked or not!"

"I'll leave the spiking to you, Mr. Applegate!" Samantha told him. "I will serve it all right by the liquor cabinet!"

Well, they'd already had their share of Christmas cookies, but Wyatt and Jessy both thanked Samantha and they all got to work.

It was nice, or should have just been a nice night, friends working together, chatting, ornaments going up, Christmas carols playing, he and Jessy singing along at times, cocoa, cookies . . .

Just a great pre-Christmas night.

But at one point, Jessy headed into the kitchen to bring some empty plates to the sink.

Wyatt was adjusting the runner on the mantel, but he saw David Benson collect one empty plate and head for the kitchen.

He followed.

But stayed behind in the hall, listening.

"Thanks, David!" Jessy said.

"Sure. Ah, nice night, really nice night. But hey, I know you're not staying."

"I haven't lied."

From his vantage point, Wyatt could see that Jessy was at the sink; David Benson was leaning on the counter by her, watching her.

"Yeah, well, I guess you need to find your grandfather's treasure first."

"His treasure?" Jessy asked. "He always considered this place, his family, and his life here at the ranch with all of you to be the best treasure any man could ask for in life."

David laughed. "Yeah, he was that kind of a guy. But he had a treasure. He always said that he wanted it for you. His granddaughter! The amazing artist!"

"Well, you know he loved my dad, first," Jessy said.

"Of course, but . . . hey, what do I know? Maybe he has some kind of treasure somewhere that only an artist would appreciate!"

"Well, I went out to see the horses tonight and had a talk with Shiloh! That horse is a treasure, for sure! Anyway, last of the dishes for now—"

"Sam usually does them, you know. If she hadn't gotten to them tonight, she'd have gotten to them in the morning. And hey, your parents can't come until tomorrow? Too bad. That's a shame."

"Yes, but they'll get here. And, in a way, I guess it will be hard for Dad, but great for him and my mom to be out here, too. Gramps would have been happy!"

"Still, you should look into that treasure thing—he talked about it now and then. Hey, who knows? Kelly

Danson was one cool guy. Maybe he had a stash of pirate gold or something like that!" David said lightly.

"David, honestly, he never, ever mentioned a treasure to me—of any kind, other than that he considered his family and his life to be the greatest treasures any man could ever want."

Wyatt frowned as he stood silently in the hallway.

Treasure?

Did David Benson really believe that there was some kind of a treasure at the ranch—and did he believe that Jessy knew about it?

Of course, Wyatt had known Kelly Danson all his life; he'd cared deeply about the man, of course—he was everything that Jessy remembered, a man who had been great to his employees, kind to everyone in the world. He'd loved horses and, of course, he survived on selling his prized quarter horses, but he never let an animal go if he doubted someone's ability to care for it well.

But as far as a physical treasure went . . .

Once, just once, Kelly had mentioned the word treasure when he talked to Wyatt, a few years back, when Jessy had still been in school. Kelly had talked about his love for his son, how gifted he was because his daughter-in-law was a true gem, and that Jessy was a true gift in life. He was a little worried, because, to a man who had worked hard and physically all his life, the pursuit of art was an "iffy" major in college and an even scarier determination for a career.

But Kelly had said, no matter what . . . well, his "treasure" would have a "treasure."

And left Wyatt there, standing in the hall eavesdropping and wondering if there was something here, hidden somewhere at the ranch, that might be considered a "treasure."

David Benson seemed to think that there was.

David laughed, standing straight. "Ah, well. It's fun to think about. You know, pirate gold, stashed somewhere and discovered!"

"Pirate gold—in Colorado. Hmm. Maybe pirates took to riding the range after they went to sea!" Jessy said lightly. "And, hey, I think we're just about done. I'm willing to bet that the house looks terrific."

"Hmm, maybe one more cocoa for me. You want another? Some tea?" David suggested.

"No, thanks. I'm going to say good night to everyone and head up soon. With the rodeo coming up and me finally deciding that I am going to ride, I want to spend the day tomorrow working with Shiloh. But thanks!" Jessy said.

Wyatt quickly moved into the kitchen.

"Oh, hey! There you are. I was starting to worry that you'd lost your way in the kitchen!" Wyatt teased.

"This one lose her way? Oh, so doubtful!" David said. "Anyway, how about you? I'm going to pour myself another from that jug of hot chocolate. You?"

"Oh, I think I had a few too many! Had a spiked one, and damn, but that Jenson Applegate knows how to pour!" Wyatt told him. "And I want to be awake and aware tomorrow, too—help Jessy get going when she works with Shiloh."

"Ah, of course! We always knew you two would end up being major lovebirds one day!" David said.

Wyatt and Jessy looked at him, startled.

David laughed.

"Yeah, you could see sparks flying when you were kids. Back then, hey, that three-year age difference was a lot. But the older you get, the less a couple of years matter, and once you guys were both teenagers, well, the sparks were flying! So, hmm. Maybe you have the magic that can keep Jessy here!" David said with a shrug. He lifted a hand. "Never mind! Don't mind me. Just the hired help!"

He headed out of the kitchen. Wyatt looked at Jessy.

Jessy looked at Wyatt.

She smiled. "Wow. I didn't know that!" she said.

He smiled back at her, but he found himself more worried than ever. The robbers who had locked Chrissie Dunworth in an underground hole and put her mother in the intensive care department had struck so many times—and were growing bolder.

What if . . .

There were too many people at the ranch. The robbers had struck empty houses, or when they knew they'd encounter perhaps just one person, easily terrified and subdued, or, as in the Dunworth case, two women who were taken entirely by surprise.

That meant that . . .

They wouldn't strike here. Because there was no way that everyone Kelly Danson had hired was a crook.

Not Cody, who had been with him since he'd been a kid. Not Samantha, not Tate . . .

But David had been around forever, too, or so it seemed. Eddie Andrews was a fairly new element in the mix, but he'd been here for several years now, too.

"Sparks, huh?" he asked her.

To his surprise, she walked over to him. "Did you know I had a crush on you when we were kids?" she asked him.

He smiled. "You were off-limits. Too young."

"Ah, but you didn't mind teasing me—turning me into a pescatarian!"

"Okay, now, that was your decision. I mean, you were petting dairy cows, so nothing was going to happen to them!"

She grinned, a hand on his chest. "You know," she told him, "they have great recording studios in New York."

He smiled at that. "It would be nice, wouldn't it?" he asked softly. "I told you and I meant it with my whole heart. I have no idea what we really were as kids—if sparks flew or whatever. I know that you were always a really great human being, just like your grandfather. Goes to show, kindness and decency can be taught. And I know that now, I'm happy to be anywhere with you."

"Hmm. So, you didn't say that you couldn't come to New York."

"I could come, but . . . my work . . ."

"The ranch?"

He laughed. "My father will have a solid hand on the

ranch for years to come. Of course, I do help out and I do travel . . ."

"You could travel to and from New York!" she said.

"It's complicated," he said simply.

Then he was grateful to be interrupted.

Cody had come into the kitchen. "I'm going out to the porch—my turn to help Misty and Morgan keep watch over the night!" he told them.

He yawned and gave himself a slight tap on the cheek.

"Just need to keep myself awake!" he said.

David Benson came in behind him.

"Cody, you've had a big day. And you're the best when it comes to helping Jessy get Shiloh in shape for the rodeo," David said. "Everyone is yawning in there. You guys can all go to bed. I'll take the night shift."

"I'm all right," Cody told him. "Wyatt is going to be helping Jessy and I'll check in on them, but he knows the horses better than I do, I think!"

"Yeah, but it's okay. My Christmas present to everyone," David said. "You guys all go and get some rest."

"I guess I should head on out," Wyatt said.

But Jessy and Cody yawned at the same time then.

And a loud alarm seemed to go off in Wyatt's head.

They'd all been together, in and out. But there had been a hell of a lot of spiked cocoa, coffee, and tea going around.

Except that . . .

Jessy hadn't had anything in her cocoa—she wanted

to be at the top of her game, riding for the first time in months, getting ready for the challenge of a barrel race.

He'd been careful himself, only pretending to drink one cup of coffee, saying that he was falling asleep without any help and wanted to get through the decorating evening.

"I'll head on out!" David said. "Oh, Wyatt, maybe—"

Wyatt made a pretense of yawning, too. "Wow. I may have to pass out on that couch in the office out in the stables," he said. "A little afraid to drive home! Wow. How the hell did we get so tired today?"

"'Tis the season!" David said lightly.

"Jess—is that okay with you? If I pass out in the stables?" Wyatt asked. "Oh, of course, Cody—"

"Fine with me," Cody said. "I just need to warn you, Wyatt, a couple of dogs may be sleeping on top of you by morning."

"No problem," Wyatt said. "Jessy?"

"Of course! You're always welcome to be here, Wyatt. Good night, then, and see you bright and early in the morning!" she said lightly, smiling at him.

"It's late for the early to bed, early to rise crew!" Cody said, laughing. "So, cool, and thanks, David."

"You got it," David said.

Wyatt nodded and turned. "I'll head out with you," David told him. "And collect the rest of those guys and get 'em out so that Sam and Jessy can get some sleep."

"Sure," Wyatt said.

"Thanks, David!" Jessy told him.

It wasn't right. Every sense in his body was telling him that something had been planned, that . . .

The hands would all be knocked out. Jessy and Samantha would be knocked out. David could do whatever he wanted to do, then feign himself as a victim of whoever had come in as well. Or . . .

Or he'd be ready with his partner—or partners—in crime to take off for an island somewhere, one that wouldn't allow extradition to the United States.

But at this moment, there wasn't a damned thing that he could prove.

He could only pretend to pass out in the stables.

"Let's call it a night!" David said as they reached the living room.

"Yeah, sad, we're hardly the last of the great partyers!" Eddie said. "And I'm still young! What the heck?"

His words were greeted with laughter. Samantha looked at Jessy and said, "Thanks for all the help. Do not pick up another thing! I swear I'll have it all cleaned up in the morning!"

"That's fine, Sam, thanks," Jessy said.

"Um, what do we do about Jenson?" Samantha asked.

The business manager was on the couch, his head leaned back.

He was snoring.

"Well, maybe you guys could stretch him out a bit—and just leave him, I guess," Jessy said.

"There's a plan!" Eddie agreed.

He went over to the sofa where Jenson Applegate was sound out; he didn't open his eyes or make a protest as Eddie and Cody tried to straighten him out so that he was lying lengthwise.

"We got it!" Eddie announced.

"Well, then . . . good night, all!" David Benson led the way out. The hands headed toward their rooms in the building behind the stables.

David took up a position on the front porch, leaned back in the chair.

"Night!" Wyatt said, heading to the stables.

He noted as he did so that Eddie Andrews paused on his way out to the rooms with Cody and Tate.

He seemed to be looking back, perplexed. But then he seemed to give himself a mental shake and move on.

Wyatt didn't switch on the lights or go to see any of the horses; the dogs, of course, wagged their tails and followed him as he headed into the office and stretched out on the sofa that was there, across from the desk.

He lay awake and waited.

A half an hour passed.

And then he heard quiet footsteps, someone tiptoeing out to make sure that he was asleep. Misty whined a bit but wagged her tail.

Wyatt remained where he lay, curled into the sofa, just letting his eyes open a slit.

And, as he'd expected, it was David Benson.

And, after checking on him, the man headed back to the house.

Wyatt waited for a beat.

And then he rose and followed.

The door opened. Jenson Applegate was standing there.

"Ready for this?" he asked David.

"Oh, hell, yes! Hell, yes!" David assured him.

And the two disappeared into the house.

CHAPTER 6

Jessy wasn't sure why she awoke.

But it seemed that her senses were instantly alert to danger.

Someone was at the door to her room; they were twisting the knob, doing it slowly, trying to do it silently.

She wasn't sure why she was so instantly alarmed. The ranch had two dogs who would go off like sirens if someone was there who shouldn't be.

But . . .

She wasn't imagining it. Someone was very furtively about to enter.

What made it so alarming she didn't know. Except that, of course, no one ever bothered her in her room. When she'd been here in days gone by, her folks or her grandfather might have knocked at her door.

Even Samantha, if she'd asked her to make sure that she was up by a certain time.

But no one ever just opened her door to come in.

She flew out of her bed and into the closet, quickly covering herself with clothing, wishing she'd had the sense to drag her purse—with her phone in it—along with her.

But as it was . . .

She had just gotten into position when the door opened fully. She heard someone enter the room.

And then swear softly.

"Where the damned hell is she?"

The speaker didn't bother to be quiet, to whisper.

Why?

Samantha might have heard, except . . .

The night had been strange. And now, of course, she knew the voice.

David Benson.

What the hell was David Benson doing, sneaking into her room in the night?

Worse. He received an answer.

"She's not here? She must be here! I watched her come up. Aw, hell, how are we going to get her and find out what the hell the treasure is without her?"

Jenson Applegate?

How was this possible?

"Did you look under the bed?" Jenson demanded, and Jessy could hear him doing so himself. "All right, I'm to go out looking. Oh, man, they're too close— maybe she's out there sleeping with the cow kid—our illustrious next-door neighbor, Wyatt McFarlane!"

"I saw her come up here!" David protested. "And I went out to see if McFarlane was really out—he's sound asleep in the stables! Alone."

"Are you sure about that?" Jenson asked.

"Damn it, yes. I saw him. I didn't see her!" David swore again.

A light went on in her room.

"Is she down the hall, in her grandfather's room . . . ? She has to have passed out by now! I checked our quarters—Tate, Cody, and Eddie are out like lights! She must have walked somewhere and then passed out," Jenson said. "Damn! We had everything all set . . . Leave it to little miss perfect New Yorker to screw everything up! All right, I'm heading down the hall!"

Jessy was still astonished.

Jenson . . . David . . . people who had worked for her grandfather for years, suddenly proving to be . . .

What?

Was it possible, could they have carried out crimes at the four corners, in the state, here . . . at the house on the outskirts of Colorado Springs?

She listened as intently as she could. The one man was leaving the room—Jenson Applegate.

And the other man, David Benson, was moving around her room, coming to the closet.

She heard him open the door, begin to shuffle through the hanging clothing. He was going to be on top of her any minute.

Suddenly, clothing shifted completely—and she was crouched in the far corner of the closet staring up at David Benson.

Not the good old boy she'd always known.

A different David Benson. A man who stared at her with pure fury and malicious intent.

"Ah, man, you screwed up! 'Cause you've seen

me now and, well . . . you should have just passed out, Jessy. We could have covered you up, masked ourselves . . . leave you to die somewhere with a little bit of hope of living—like that Chrissie girl! Well—" He broke off and reached for her.

"Touch her and you're a dead man!"

Startled, David Benson straightened.

"I've got a Glock 19 trained at your head and I know how to use it really well!"

Jessy swallowed hard.

The man was just staring at her. He had a gun, she realized, tucked into a holster held at his left side on his belt.

He stared at her.

And reached for the gun.

She heard the explosion of a bullet; David Benson screamed in agony.

But he was alive, falling back, grabbing the left side of his body. He staggered forward; for a moment, she thought that he was going to fall on her.

She shoved him back and he stumbled, falling backward, falling flat with a tremendous crashing sound.

She jumped out of the closet, stunned anew.

Apparently, Wyatt didn't trust the man, even shot through the hand and the hip; he had hunkered down by him with small plastic strips that looked like something that might close a food storage bag—but they were handcuffs, she realized.

He cuffed the man while pulling out his phone, hitting a number and quickly announcing to whoever answered where he was and what was happening. But as he did so, she saw Jenson Applegate appear at the door.

And he was armed.

And aiming his gun at Wyatt's head.

She would never know what propelled her at that moment—she usually thought of herself as pretty much a coward.

But everything that had happened in the last few minutes had been stunning, terrifying, surreal . . .

And so was the move she made.

Shrieking like a banshee, she propelled herself at Jenson. She did so with such force that the two of them went crashing to the ground.

The man's gun went off.

But she wasn't hit; neither was Wyatt. Jenson's bullet soared upward with the speed of light and hit the ceiling, creating another shattering sound as the man's gun went sliding far across the room.

She was on top of Jenson.

He stared at her furiously, shoving at her and trying to get his hands around her neck.

Not a chance.

Wyatt caught hold of Jessy, lifting her far from the man. And when Jenson tried to rise after her in his fury, Wyatt caught him with a solid blow to the chin that sent the man reeling back to the floor with a thud.

He'd holstered his own gun; he seemed to know what he was doing. In a flash, he had taken out a second set of the baggie-tie-looking cuffs, and they were on the man.

By then, David was bellowing in pain, claiming that

Wyatt was a monster, that he was the one who had orchestrated everything; they had just been trying to save her because they knew that he was on the property.

"Too late, David. I remember every word that you said to me when you found me in the closet," Jessy told him.

And then, even though they were on a ranch—far from a crowded area—she heard sirens in the night.

And in seconds, officers—in uniform and not—were spilling into the house. One female officer wanted to know if she had been assaulted, if she wanted to go to the hospital.

No, no, no. She didn't want to go to the hospital.

And, of course, it was amazing that with all the commotion . . .

"Samantha!" she said, and she swept through the law enforcement in the ranch house and hurried to Samantha's room.

The housekeeper still appeared to be sound asleep.

"She's been drugged; they slipped it into the coffee and cocoa and everything we had tonight," Wyatt said from behind her. He looked over at one of the officers in plainclothes and said, "We need medical attention out here—"

"EMTs on the way. And there's an ambulance waiting for the fellow you shot—don't worry, Miss Danson, McFarlane, he'll be arrested and read his rights on the way," the man told him.

The man seemed to know Wyatt and know him well. Jessy made sure that Samantha was breathing; she was.

She seemed fine. Except that she didn't wake up. She made a little noise and adjusted her position when Jessy tried to wake her.

"She'll be all right, I believe."

Jessy turned. She studied the man in plainclothes who seemed to be in charge. He was tall, bald, in excellent physical shape, and wearing a suit. He was a man, she thought, in control of any situation he encountered.

And Wyatt seemed to know him, too.

He turned from Jessy to Wyatt. "The others are checking on the men down in their living quarters. From seeing this woman, I believe they'll be all right. But more ambulances, as I said, are on the way."

"Thank you," Wyatt told him.

"They'll get the injured man first, of course."

"Right, I might have completely shattered his hip. No choice. He was drawing a gun," Wyatt said. "His gun is back in Jessy's room—flew up and across the bed when I shot him—and Jenson Applegate's gun is at the far side of her room, by the wall. Jessy tackled him when he was about to shoot me in the head. He still tried to strangle her."

"CSU will be in here, but you know the drill—"

"Yes, sir, I know the drill," Wyatt said, handing his own weapon over to the man.

And it was suddenly too much.

"Who *are* you?" Jessy demanded, staring at Wyatt.

He closed his eyes for a second, wincing. "I'm sorry, Jessy. I've been working on these robberies undercover. This gentleman is SSA Vargas, my supervisor."

"And you, miss, are quite an amazing young woman," Vargas said, nodding appreciatively to her. "First, you find a young woman that three different law enforcement agencies couldn't find, and now . . ."

"You saved my life," Wyatt told her.

She still frowned, confused. "Working undercover?"

"Wyat is with the bureau, has been for years," Vargas told her. "He's one of our best, and in this instance, he was incredibly useful undercover with his own identity since he's from here, knows the area, knows the people . . . and anyway, I'm sorry, but after all this, we need to bring you in to give your statement. And you're sure you're all right? We can make sure that you receive medical attention—"

"No, no, I don't need medical attention! But . . . well, we never just leave the ranch, and if Samantha and the others are at the hospital or being arrested—"

"Right now, the ranch is a crime scene. We'll have agents here," Vargas promised her. He smiled. "We won't keep you long. We know you endured a very long day already."

Well, there was one thing that was good; she hadn't been drugged because she'd only pretended to enjoy snacks and drinks with their friends.

Apparently, Wyatt had done the same.

Because he'd been on duty. He'd been working. Of course, that was a good thing—she had no idea what might have happened to her if he hadn't been there to stop David Benson and Jenson Applegate.

But had anything between them been real? On her part, yes.

But he had been working undercover! Were the little moments of intimacy they had shared nothing more than a necessary act?

No real chance to think about it then.

She gathered her things, opting to drive into Colorado Springs with one of the agents she had met the night before, leaving Wyatt and his superior to drive in together.

She wasn't put through any kind of a drill; she simply described exactly what had happened. She didn't know all that much about law enforcement—federal or local—but she assumed that Wyatt was doing whatever an agent had to do when criminals had been stopped but one had been shot in the process.

When she was finished, she was glad to see that he wasn't in an outer room, waiting.

When she was offered a ride home, she opted for a ride to the hospital instead.

She had to find out how Cody, Samantha, Tate, and Eddie were doing.

She was able to speak with a doctor who told her that they were still doing blood tests but that the group brought in was doing well; each one of them was in stable condition, and from various cases he'd worked before, they might have been dosed with a mixture of cocaine—and alcohol.

Well, Jenson Applegate had been pouring the drinks. Friendly, pleasant, having a good old time . . .

And possibly the last person anyone might suspect.

But she needed to know that her people would be fine. At the moment, though . . .

To use a truly professional term, the doctor told her dryly, they were all still *loopy*.

And still, she went to check on everyone. And it was Cody, confused—loopy—fighting for his sense of reason, who told her that he should have suspected something; David Benson had been bad about arriving for shifts on time. He'd taken to staying out all night in the last months, hinting that he had a new love in his life.

But he'd also been convinced, once Kelly Danson had left to head east to be with his family in his final days, that Kelly had left a treasure behind. A treasure that would go to his granddaughter.

"The treasure is the ranch!" Cody whispered. "The ranch, the house, the horses, the stables . . . How could I have worked with people for so many years, and not known?"

Jessy tried to calm him, telling him that they were lucky it had worked out the way that it had.

Lucky, because Wyatt McFarlane had been there.

Determined not to drink so that he could help her get ready for the rodeo.

Maybe it was a really good thing that her parents hadn't managed to get a flight yet.

She managed to see Samantha, Eddie, and Tate for just a few minutes, time to assure them that they were going to be all right, they'd be coming home soon.

Then the agent assigned to her assured her that the crime scene units had finished at her house; she could go home if she chose, and they'd have an agent keeping watch over everything until her people were able to come home.

She was assured with the evidence they'd accrued against Benson and Applegate that the men would be remanded. They would not be out for years and years.

She was fine.

She wanted to go home.

At the house, she went to see the dogs where they were keeping guard in the stables. She didn't blame them.

They hadn't known those they considered to be friends were the enemy.

Neither had she.

But . . .

How much had Wyatt known? What had he suspected?

Second night, little or no sleep. She didn't go upstairs; she crashed out on the couch where Jenson Applegate had pretended to be just as knocked out as the rest of the household.

She slept, despite the tug-of-war going on in her mind. And when she woke up, Wyatt McFarlane was sitting in one of the parlor's armchairs, watching her.

She sat up immediately, staring at him.

"Wyatt, you don't need to be here anymore. You caught your crooks. I mean, man, I'm sorry as hell that it was here. I still can't believe that these men worked for my grandfather for years, and . . ."

"I believe it was when your grandfather first became ill that they started on this. And I'll be honest—I had no clue until I heard Cody talking to David one day," Wyatt explained.

"Look, I'm exceedingly glad that they've been caught! I do believe that they would have killed me if you hadn't been here—"

"Hey, Jenson Applegate could have shot me. What you did was incredibly foolhardy and brave and still . . . he could have shot you, and that horrifies me, and on the other hand, he could have killed me—"

"If you hadn't been there, I would have died. The idiots were convinced that my grandfather had some kind of treasure stashed here and that I must know what it was and where it was. But there is no treasure, and they weren't the brightest of criminals because, seriously, how could they guarantee that all of us would be out cold? They couldn't, but they have been getting away with it for a while, so they must have studied up on how to manage a crime and leave no evidence. But the point is, Wyatt, they've been caught. You don't need to—"

She was startled when he moved over to the couch, sitting beside her, taking her hand and speaking to her earnestly.

"Jessy, Jessy, it killed me not to tell you the truth! And it amazed me, of course, that you were the one who didn't give up on Chrissie, who was determined when the rest of us couldn't find a building anywhere near the house where she might have been stashed away. And you found her. You've been a far superior law enforcement agent and you're not in law enforcement at all. But Jessy . . ."

For a minute, his voice trailed.

"Jessy, I swear to you, every second I was with you . . . all I wanted to do was be with you!"

He sounded so honest, so sincere.

But she was still reeling. She stood.

"Jessy?"

"I'm going to go and take Shiloh through his paces. The rodeo is coming up," she told him. "Excuse me. I know you're an agent and that agents are supposedly watching over me until others return, but you really don't need to stay—"

"Jessy, the rodeo isn't the end of the world, you know. If you—"

"I can see little more important right now than getting my horse up to speed. Excuse me."

"I'll help."

"I don't need you—"

"But I need you . . . the rodeo . . . horse . . . bulls."

She headed out. He followed her.

And as it happened, they worked through the afternoon. Worked, and as they did so, Jessy remembered everything about riding, weight distribution, heels down, feeling the animal beneath you, know your horse, his every movement.

Bizarrely, it was a good afternoon.

At last, when she cooled Shiloh down and brushed him after their hours working at the paddock, she realized that she hadn't told her parents anything.

They would hear about it on the news, she was afraid!

"What's wrong?" Wyatt asked her.

"My folks are coming soon. And . . ."

"Call them. Hey, I called mine first chance I got," Wyatt told her.

"But they know what you do, right?"

He shrugged.

"Pity you couldn't have shared that info with me!"

He shrugged, shaking his head. "Jessy . . . never mind. I guess it's asking too much for you to forgive me."

She didn't reply. She made a call through to her father, making it all as light as she could. But, of course, he was in shock—he'd known all his father's employees forever and ever, too, and he was stunned and distraught.

She realized that Wyatt could see she was having trouble with the call. He reached for her phone with a brow arched high.

And she listened. Well, he'd gotten good at telling the truth—with a twist. They'd been in control the entire time. Jessy was a heroine to all in the region. She was amazing.

"Well!" her father said, when she had the phone again. "Thank God for Wyatt!"

"Uh, yeah."

At last, she was able to end the call. She wouldn't be picking them up at the airport until five Friday. She tried to talk more about the horses, assuring her father that he and her mom would have fun—they'd get there just in time for the rodeo, an art show opening, and Christmas!

When she ended the call at last, Wyatt was watching her.

"Okay, it's all good. You really can leave now," she told him.

He shook his head. "I can just sit on the porch if you like."

"Fine. Suit yourself," she told him.

Jessy realized that they hadn't eaten. They were both exhausted, of course, but . . . well, if they were hungry, they'd wake up once they'd fallen asleep.

She went on into the kitchen and found that Samantha had seen that they were well supplied with tuna and salmon.

She started preparing dinner: salmon, peas, corn, and rice.

The whole time she was cooking, she didn't see Wyatt. When the meal was prepared at last, she headed out to the porch.

"Um, I cooked. You did save my life. I guess you could eat."

"Well, since you saved my life, too, I'll be grateful to eat while I'm alive!" he told her.

He left the chair and followed her into the house. They ate in the kitchen, quiet for most of the meal. Toward the end, however, he swore softly.

"I'll be back."

"Where are you going?"

"The animals! They all need to be fed."

"Oh, my God! I'm horrible. My grandfather never should have trusted this place to me in any way, shape, or form! I need to do that—"

"Stop! You fed us, I'll feed them. Remember, son of a rancher, you know."

"Undercover cowboy!" she said sweetly.

He winced and headed out. After a while, she followed him. He was finished with the last of his hay dumps and looked at her. Of course, Misty and Morgan were all over them, and she petted the dogs and looked at him and said, "Thank you."

"Dinner was great. Maybe I could be a pescatarian," he told her. "And don't worry, I'll be on the porch all night."

She'd known him all her life, in a way, she thought. She'd just been so stunned. And then . . .

So hurt and confused, grateful, and wounded and wondering, what was part of work, what was part of all that everyone seemed to think existed between the two of them.

Did it matter? She was an adult. She'd head back to New York when she damned well felt like it. Life here had become unexpectedly and ridiculously traumatic. She was in no condition to make important decisions, but . . .

"You don't have to stay on the porch. You're welcome to come in."

"I should—"

"I'm not blind. There's a car down at the property line—one of your fellows has been looking over this place all day. And you're not officially working, I know. You handed in your gun and badge to be cleared in the shooting."

He smiled. "You watch too much TV," he told her.

She smiled sweetly. "Not really. I have a lot of books! The point being, you're welcome to stay in the house. I know you're not officially working."

He shrugged. "Okay. Thank you."

"Or go home."

"I still just . . ." He broke off, shaking his head. "I still just need to know that you're safe."

She smiled, nodded, and headed up the stairs. She really needed a shower.

But in the shower, she kept thinking and thinking.

Of course, everything in the last hours had been ridiculous and amazing, so . . .

She stepped out of the shower, wrapping herself up in a towel. Wincing inwardly, she knew what she was about to do. But she couldn't stop herself. Real or not, she didn't want to disbelieve all that had grown between them.

She had promised that their kissing would be continued.

And so, in her towel, she headed down the stairs. He'd been reading one of her grandfather's books on World War II, but when she appeared, he looked up, frowning.

"You need a shower. Badly," she told him.

His frown deepened. "But—"

"Seriously!"

Curiously, he set the book down and rose.

"Jessy, I'd never rush you, I'd never push you . . . I mean, I know you're angry, but I really had no choice, but the thing of it is, I swear, every minute with you—"

"Please! Just get in the shower!"

He hurried up the stairs, stopping in front of her.

"Get in, please!" she said.

He did so.

And she dropped her towel and stepped in behind him, slipping her arms around him, laying her cheek against his back and just holding on for a minute.

She felt his heartbeat, felt his strength. And when he turned to her, she knew—she understood—it had hurt him worse than it was hurting her now to keep the truth from her. She smiled, and when they kissed, it seemed like an eternal kiss, as if all pretense was washed away within the heat of their lips and fall of the water.

And then they were both able to smile, tease with words and lips and fingertips, determined that they wouldn't fall and break their necks in the shower, that they could and would continue these kisses.

And so, they did.

It felt like lying with him was something she had waited for, wanted all of her life.

And then . . .

That night, they slept together.

Of course, when the staff returned the following day, an hour ensued of everyone being incredulous, horrified, and gratified that they were all alive.

And hailing their heroes.

Apparently the plan had been to spirit Jessy away

and hold her far into an old field until she gave up the "treasure." They'd have come back to the property themselves to have been drugged by the kidnappers as well.

Now . . . they'd all just be waiting for a court date.

Jessy still managed to work with Shiloh quite a bit before she and Wyatt were headed for the airport at last.

Samantha, insisting she was just fine, wanted to create a wonderful feast for Jessy, Wyatt, Jessy's folks—and Wyatt's folks.

And she did. So, despite more talk about the robberies and what had happened at the ranch, it was a strangely good night. One that apparently let both sets of parents realize that their children were . . . a duo.

The next day was even better.

Wyatt took the bull riding championship and Jessy won in the barrel racing category.

Sunday, they were off to the art show, the gallery opening. And Jessy discovered that she loved the owner who knew her work and was in love with it.

He wanted to do a showcase of her work. Well, of course, if she was going to determine a time when she was going to be out there, and they could arrange a date.

Wyatt had time off; he and the band accepted an offer to play at Murphy's Pub on Christmas Eve and so their families all joined them as well, and with friends and others, they filled the place—making Brian Murphy very happy.

Jessy did "What Child Is This?" with Wyatt again, making their parents very happy as well.

It was Christmas morning when Wyatt arrived, anxious to see her as soon as possible. Jessy had determined that the hands were going to have the day off—entirely off—and Wyatt was helping her feed all the livestock.

Extra hay for Christmas!

And when she shoved aside one of the dividers, that was when she found her grandfather's "treasure."

Others might not have recognized the painting. It was of a small boy. A shimmering halo was above his head and his hands were folded in prayer while bombs exploded around him.

She hadn't realized that Wyatt had come in behind her until she heard his exclamation.

"Oh, wow! My lord, it can't be—"

She spun on him. "You know what that is? I mean, if it's real, but I think that it is!"

"The missing Markel. It's called *Halo*."

Not even all those who had studied art for years knew about Michael Markel, an artist who had worked in Germany during World War II, escaping just before he might have spent his final days in a camp.

He'd done ten famous paintings about the war.

And . . . at the end of the war, the whereabouts of one had been unknown while others sat in art museums around the world.

"How do you know—" she began.

He smiled at her. "Your grandfather's book. He collected so many. And it all makes sense. Who else should have such a 'treasure,' who else but an artist to truly appreciate the meaning of the piece above the value of the piece!"

"Well, it's going to need to hang in the house! I wonder why he kept it out here. Oh, and the odd thing is—"

"That David and Jenson saw it several times, at least, and never had any idea that they knew exactly where a treasure could be found."

She smiled. She walked up to him, curling her arms around his neck and looking into his eyes.

"I know something that they would never understand," she said softly.

He smiled. "What's that?" he asked her.

"This painting is *a* treasure. But I don't think it was *the* treasure my grandfather might have meant for me."

"Oh?"

"You're my treasure!" she said softly.

"And mine forever. Here, New York, I can transfer . . . uh, I don't have a diamond yet, but . . ."

"Are you asking me to marry you?" she demanded.

"Uh, yeah. Not really horribly romantic, here in a feed shed, but . . ."

She laughed softly. "I'm in."

"But I thought that all you really wanted was to get back to the city for Christmas—"

She pressed her fingers to his lips, shaking her head.

"I've found real treasure. Grandfather left it for me. I just had to realize what it was!" she told him.

"And I swear, with every ounce of me, for all of my life . . . if you're finding me to be part of this treasure . . .

well, you've got this one! And seriously, for all of our lives!"

Christmas.

She would always miss her grandfather. And even having passed on . . .

Even with the trauma of the robbers . . .

Kelly Danson had managed to leave her pure treasure, the best Christmas present ever!